*IF FOUND,*
*PLEASE RETURN TO*

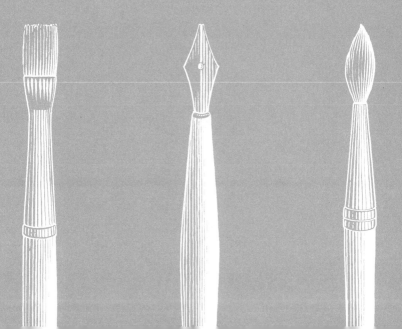

# ALL
# THE
# COLOUR
# IN
# THE
# WORLD

*A Novel*

## CS RICHARDSON

*Alfred A. Knopf Canada*

Library and Archives Canada Cataloguing in Publication

Title: All the colour in the world / CS Richardson.
Names: Richardson, CS, author.
Identifiers: Canadiana (print) 20220235082 | Canadiana (ebook) 2022023521X |
ISBN 9781039003514 (hardcover) | ISBN 9781039003521 (EPUB)
Classification: LCC PS8635.I325 A75 2023 | DDC C813/.6—dc23

Jacket and text design: Kelly Hill
Jacket images: Front: George Marks/Getty Images; Spine: *The Schoolboy*,
Vincent van Gogh/Artvee; Back: *Dort or Dordrecht—The Dort Packet-Boat
from Rotterdam Becalmed*, JMW Turner/Artvee; Flaps: *Still Life*, Henri
Fantin-Latour/Artvee; Paint: (cadmium yellow) Elen11, (vermilion)
TanyaRow, (teal) SvitlanaMartyn, all from Getty Images; (cinabrese)
Alexander, (British racing green) Krakenimages.com,
(Cambridge blue) elen31, all Adobe Stock Images
Interior image credits: *Odalisque in Grisaille*, Jean Auguste Dominique
Ingres, The Metropolitan Museum of Art, New York; Sunnyside
Boardwalk Toronto 1931, Wikimedia Commons; Old illustration
of Lettuce Rose (Rosa centifolia bullata). Created by P.R. Redoute,
published on Les Roses, Imp. Firmin Didot, Paris, 1817–24 by
Mannaggia/Adobe Stock; (paintbrush) channarongsds/Getty images
Endpaper: (cinabrese) Alexander/Adobe Stock Images; (paintbrush)
channarongsds/Getty images

Printed in Canada

10 9 8 7 6 5 4 3 2

Penguin
Random House
KNOPF CANADA

For Rebecca, *certo*.

Art is seed, art is memory, art is vaccine.

YANN MARTEL, *Beatrice & Virgil*

Employing *zuihitsu*, a Japanese writing style characterized by both linked essays and disparate ideas, Sei Shōnagon considers her *Pillow Book*—a collection of anecdotes, musings about life as a courtier, favourite quotations, poetry, lists, daily affirmations—to be for her eyes only.

In Renaissance Italy such a personal almanac is known as a *zibaldone*: an informal miscellany containing everything from landscape sketches to currency exchange rates, medicinal recipes to family trees. The Florentine politician and merchant Giovanni Rucellai likens his to "a salad of many herbs."

Such salads might fill otherwise blank scrap albums, pocket journals, or composition books. One could just as easily find them straining the bindings of pre-existing books, a time-worn university text, perhaps.

Consider your beginning.

Father in ill-fitting tweeds, waiting for an eastbound street-car, worrying the coins in his pocket. Mother clinging to his remaining arm, her best cotton dress (generous with the letting out) billowing in the heat rising from the pavement. She carries low, a month early, knees buckling six minutes on the tick.

The morning editions, brash with their 60-points, predict another dog day, the hottest of the summer.

The indifferent vise of contraction tightens. Five minutes now. You could set your watch.

The streetcar is nowhere to be seen. In your parents' rising panic, the thought of giving birth in a stifling walk-up in the Shoreview Mansions grips each in a private nightmare.

Mother pictures herself flat on her back, a beached whale gasping on the parlour floor. Curses loud and blue, legs splayed for all to see, mysterious fluids ruining the rug. One floor below, her mother-in-law (soon enough Gran) dimples her ceiling with a broom handle, trying to silence the frankly unnecessary language coming from above.

Father remembers other leavings of the human body: the thick red violence of it all, no matter that present (if pressing) circumstances might be considered more an affirmation, less a taking, of life.

Teetering at the curb, Mother's fingers claw at her husband's sleeve. She loses count, starts again. One Piccadilly, two Piccadilly.

Father's tweeds: a mix of russet and umber. Mother's dress: cerulean. The sky: murky, Turneresque, awash with Indian yellow.

The Dutch East Indies, spring 1815. On the island of Sumbawa, Mount Tambora erupts. The resulting cloud of ash, ten times the debris that buried Pompeii, circles the globe, creating a variety of optical phenomena. Prolonged sunsets colour European skies throughout the summer and fall. Abnormal twilights glow orange and red near the horizon, ethereal purple and pink above. Daylight skies appear muddy, as though skim-coated with yellow. Temperatures cool, triggering extreme fluctuations in weather. 1816 becomes the Year Without a Summer.

Meanwhile the artist J.M.W. Turner works his way through another sketching book—he will eventually fill 290 such volumes with pencilled scribbles, hasty watercolour impressions, and detailed notations concerning the play of light and colour in the natural world. This particular sketchbook concentrates on the optics of the English sky, including the colour anomalies caused by the Tambora eruption.

In finished paintings such as *Chichester Canal* (1828), Turner will move easily from sketch to canvas, putting the vermilions, the chrome oranges, the Indian yellows of his observations to characteristically evocative use.

Mother's pregnancy is her first: a natural (one might argue predictable) denouement to an evening that occurs eight months earlier; an evening prologued by a day spent on a station platform pacing holes in her best stockings, at last to see a mirage of Brasso'd buttons and hollowed cheeks, pressed khaki and sunken eyes, step lively from a third-class carriage.

6.

Discharge paperwork, awkwardly left-handed, in Ypres. Back-of-a-lorry to Le Havre, steerage to Quebec, third-class to Toronto. The run along the platform, the warm, wet kisses of his wife.

And despite leaving an arm amid the stumps of Sanctuary Wood—hot shrapnel cleaving the wing mid-humerus, relegating surgeons to crimp-and-hem like so much piecework—Father brings home a certain (boudoir) expertise.

(Acquired on the frayed edges of Bailleul.)

(In the instructive embraces of one Mademoiselle Lillian.)

(Known to both sides of the salient as Lily L'Azure.)

As unsettling as the mental pictures may be, you imagine your parents' homecoming evening as one of abandon: Mother, décolletage brushed in the reddish flush of intimacy, keeps a sweaty grip on bedstead and discretion, directs Father's pruned acrobatics with gentle patience; resists asking where (or for that matter how) he learned to do such things with touch and tongue.

Do not question such diplomacy. The woman's heart is returned when so many are left to fertilize the charnel muck of Flanders.

Returned in more or less one piece.

(Returned, as Lillian might purr, with such *jouissance*.)

Occupied by German forces since the earliest days of the First World War, the French town of Bailleul is liberated by British, Australian, and Canadian troops in October 1914. Located a leisurely half-day march across the nearby Belgian frontier to the trenches surrounding Ypres, the town is transformed into a base for Allied actions along the front.

Bailleul's asylum, established in 1863 as a psychiatric hospital for women, dubbed the Red Asylum because of its exterior brickwork, is home to more than a thousand patients. The British army commandeers the building, converting it to a military hospital and soldiers' recreation facility complete with swimming pool, hot showers, and laundry.

There is speculation that, as the British moved in, some of the thousand may have chosen to remain in the care of the asylum's nuns. Others may have opted for a fresh madness: a return to life on the outside, albeit in a war zone.

They may have returned as mothers, as wives, as daughters. As schoolteachers, shopgirls, barmaids. Perhaps a few as the town's *filles de joie*.

German forces recapture Bailleul in April 1918. Until its liberation three months later, it is shelled almost daily; more than 100,000 rounds fall on the town. Ninety-eight percent of its structures—including schools, cafés, brothels—are destroyed.

The Red Asylum begins rebuilding in 1922. There is no record of how many of the thousand returned.

Would a mention of Lillian's *nom d'amour* spark a glow amid Father's darkest memories? Would he risk an enigmatic grin when recalling the inviting cyans of mademoiselle's intimates?

However muddied, bloodied, and far from home he was when in said boudoir, picturing him helping Mother's feet to find the streetcar's boarding step, you trust he would remain a gentleman.

Mum would be the word.

## II

The streetcar pulls away: Mother hovering her nether regions above a forward seat. The longest journey of her young life ends downtown at a small hospital shoehorned into what was once the home of some city grandee.

While an attending nurse takes note of particulars, the admitting doctor pulls aside her mask, offers Mother a smile. Fear not, the doctor says, there's nothing here we haven't seen before.

Mother gives in to the doctor's knowing pokes-and-prods; gives in to exhaustion, gives in to deliverance.

The Ontario Medical College for Women opens a small clinic in 1895. The facility offers patients the services of female doctors practising a discipline that at the time is almost exclusively male. Medical care is provided regardless of a patient's ability to pay.

The College combines the clinic with a small hospital in 1911. A modest operation of seven beds, it is officially designated as the Women's College Hospital & Dispensary two years later.

In short order the WCH&D outgrows its first location, opening a new hospital four years later. Spread over three floors of a former private residence, the 25-bed facility includes ten cots for children.

The WCH&D is meticulous:
    —umbilical neatly clamped and trimmed;
    —pounds and ounces (seven and six) duly noted;
    —digits (times twenty) double-counted;
    —mushy cranium measured with tailor's tape;
    —complexion checked against reference swatches
      (stillborn greys to healthy pinks);
    —swaddling tucked with origamic precision;
    —orderlies prompt with the mopping up;
    —Father frogmarched from a hallway then reprimanded
      for the state of his remaining fingernails.

Africa hot, boast the evening editions. 72-point.

31 August 1916. Happy birthday.

The smells of a first memory: suppertime.

You (at three?) perched on the family sofa (blue with yellow flowers? itchy woollen fabric?), feet in holed socks dangling above the floor; outstretched legs cradling a toy sailboat. Skull-and-bone sails, black hull.

Father arrives home, flops down beside you, calls to Mother. Isn't it nice to know, he says, that everyone loves a veteran as long as the fellow has all his bits BUT if he chokes enough on his starched collar and tugs enough at his forelock there might be a situation next week, nothing permanent mind you, clerking if that suits, no guarantees, try back tomorrow. When's supper?

Father flattens his armless sleeve around you, loosens his tie, clears his throat. Time enough for a story, then, he says, launching into a tale he will tell so often that you will know it by heart, his good arm lifting your boat over invisible waves. A tale of peg-legged pirates and a ship appearing through the fog. Of Spaniards and sailing off the edge of the world.

Red sky at night? Father says. Sailor's delight, you reply.

Mother summons you both to the kitchen.

As for your fifth birthday, a family meeting. Father pacing, Gran's fists balling the furniture doilies, Mother sitting mute. You industrious: doodling in a corner, mumbling to yourself.

The lad—if he stops his chatterboxing—should expect honest labour, Father says. Torn knuckles and bad knees and a strong back for his troubles, a steady wage and food in his belly. He'll apprentice, he'll learn the trade, before you know it he'll be bricking fifty feet of road in a day. And he'll do it without so much as a peep.

Leave the lad alone, Gran says. The apple will fall where it finds better light, whether you like it or not. In the meantime, I should think five is a little young to be putting the lad to work.

Mother, eight months pregnant, glares at Father. He won't be your lad forever, she says.

Father's eyes go dark. As the master, so the man, he says, with two good arms, damn him.

And you will be a man before learning that small, bony-handed Gran—living one floor below, smelling of lemons and the occasional whiskey—arrived in your life with something of a history.

Since you've asked, Gran will say.

She will tell you she was born in an end-of-terrace in Tullamore, never-you-mind when. That a steamer out of Belfast brought her across the ocean. That she hated the grey winters, missed the green of home, dutifully memorized her Thomas Moore, worked hard at her classics, became a teacher: English, grammar, composition.

That when the form inquired as to religion, she wrote *Irish*. That she refused to swallow her brogue, knowing full well she might better advance without it. That she joined a literary club, knowing full well she was as clever as anyone else in the room.

Young ladies seeking membership in the Toronto Women's Literary Club (founded in 1876) do so—as far as their prying menfolk need know—so they might a) widen their intellectual horizon, b) engage in discussions of the literary or scientific arts, c) attend the occasional guest lecture, or d) get out of the house once in a while and make new friends.

If these new friends turn out to be women prone to more vigorous thinking, women perfectly willing to set the cat among the pigeons and turn enlightened conversation into calls to action—securing a sister's right to economic independence, say, or declaring a sister's status equal to any man's, or marching for a sister's political freedom—then the member candidate joins the Club at her own risk.

In 1883, celebrating a partial victory in achieving the vote for women (partial in that a woman wishing to cast a ballot must be both single *and* a property owner), the TWLC lets said cat out of the bag and renames the organization the Canadian Women's Suffrage Association.

Gran will speak of a hard January freeze-and-thaw playing havoc with her school's masonry, and, come spring, the need for repointing. Of falling in love with the handsome mason pulling faces at her through her classroom window. Of the mason dying a year later, a distracted step, a fall from a scaffold. Of being pregnant with their son, your father.

Gran will turn away, her breath catching. He wasn't always angry, your father, she will say. He learned his letters and numbers like any mother's son, but he never took to books. He was his father's son. He liked working with his hands.

Apples and trees, Gran will say.

A month later, you find yourself dragged back to the WCH&D in best navy serge and starched collar. Mother has again given birth.

Father nestles a sleeping croissant of blankets in the crook of his one arm. Our Lizzie, he says, grin toothy and wide.

Wee Bess, Mother says.

Gran look to you, lifts an expectant eyebrow, misquotes her Shakespeare: as a brother to his sister, show bashful sincerity and comely love.*

The serge chafes, the collar chokes, Gran rephrases: wipe that scowl off your face and introduce yourself as the proud big brother or, make no mistake, hell will hath no fury like a woman scorned.†

---

* *Much Ado about Nothing*, act iv scene 1; Claudio to Leonato, regarding Hero.
† *The Mourning Bride*, act iii scene 2. William Congreve, not Shakespeare at all. Nonetheless, point taken.

Ferrara, summer 1519. A noblewoman delivers her tenth child, a stillborn girl. The mother, Lucrezia Borgia, quickly develops childbed fever. She is dead within ten days.

Vienna, late in the 1840s. Obstetrician and teacher Ignaz Semmelweis ponders a theory. Could some sort of bacterial infection cause the childbed fever that is killing a fifth of his postpartum mothers? He instructs his students to wash their hands *before* examining an expectant patient.

Paris, a decade later. Louis Pasteur compares the hygiene practices of the city's maternity wards with their relative rates of childbed fever. A stickler for a more professional nomenclature, Pasteur prefers the term *sepsis*, from the Greek "to make rotten."

It is soon clear that the WCH&D staff have studied the work of their forebears. They are well aware that perfect hygiene—no matter the crispness of the nurses' bib-and-cap, the diligence of the orderlies, the cleanliness of one's fingernails—is as unattainable as the Grail.

Three days after your introduction to Bess, the word *sepsis* appears on Mother's death certificate.

Father brings Bess home to the Shoreview. Leaving you both to Gran's care, he shuts himself in what fate has turned into a widower's flat. It is a week before he reappears: a phantom, pasty and grey, stumbling over another meal gathering flies on the landing.

You watch from the top of the stairwell. Father's descending steps search for footing, his untied boots hovering in mid-air as though the hangman has just opened the trap.

To produce natural vermilion, cinnabar (a by-product of mercury mining) is ground to a powder, thereby creating an unpredictable range of warm hues, from bright orange-red to dark reddish purple. These colour differences are caused in part by the coarseness of the grind: the larger the particles, the duller the hue. In any event, the resulting powder is poisonous.

Fortunately, the Chinese begin producing a synthetic vermilion in the fourth century BCE. Their recipe is simple: mix mercury and sulphur to form a black compound, mercury sulphide; heat the compound then vaporize and re-condense; grind the result to a powder, thus changing the black to red. The finer the grind, the brighter the hue. As harmless as baking flour.

Seventeenth-century Europe updates the Chinese process: heat the mercury sulphide in a retort; condense the resulting vapours into red sulphide crystals; remove the lethal sulphur by treating the crystals with an alkali; rinse; grind under water. Mixing the resulting power with binders such as oil or egg tempera can produce an artist's vivid sunset, a tempting apple, or a remarkable shade of lipstick.

As Father reaches the bottom of the stairs, Gran bends to your ear and whispers. You oblige with a salute.

What remains of Father touches the peak of his cap, his eyes staring past you. He turns, disappearing into the setting glare of a vermilion sun.

You look to Gran. We mustn't worry, you say.

Why is that, dear boy?

Red sky at night.

You fight the urge to close your eyes. Comes that early memory: the reek of over-boiled vegetables.

Suppertime: Mother summons you and Father to the kitchen. Elbows off the table, she says, placing a plated grey-green mound in front of you. Runny mashed potatoes, limp cabbage, a bit of onion, a bit of mealy sausage. You make a face. Hush, Mother says. It's Saturday pie, your favourite.

Even at this age, you know your pie: when Gran makes pie, the whole Shoreview smells like cinnamon; when Mother makes pie, it looks nothing like pie. She claims that pickings have been slim at the market these days.

Father slides away the slop. I need some air, he says.

Footfalls down the stairs, a door slamming. Shall we practise our letters? Mother says.

*A was an Archer, who shot at a frog,*
*B was a Butcher, who had a great dog.*

You are shy to act out the characters. You stumble through *L*, *M*, *N*, put *Q* before *P*, forget *T*. Behind her hand, Mother stage-whispers her prompts. You close—*Z was a Zany, who looked a great fool*—with a stiff bow from the waist. Mother jumps to her feet.

Your cheeks go hot, your forehead breaks out in a nervous sweat. Heaven forbid the neighbours might hear Mother's bravos.

In the weeks following Father's disappearance you begin confiding in yourself, trying to ease the knot in your stomach, telling yourself tales of a young prince pacing the castle walls alone, waiting for the return of his absent King and Queen.

The prince listens for the sound of untied boots taking the stairs two at a time. Gone silent are the King's night terrors, loud enough to wake the castle.

The prince sniffs to catch a trace of lavender soap before the Queen opens his bedroom door. Gone silent are her assurances to the King: the rats have moved on, the guns gone still.

Your mumbling catches Gran's ear. No shame in keeping yourself company, she says. Shakespeare's lot do it with surprising regularity.

You will eventually dismiss these private stories. You were only five, after all. The *sotto voce*, however, will linger a lifetime.

The first rowing contest between Oxford and Cambridge universities takes place in 1829. The Oxford Eight wear white shirts striped with a deep azure blue (the boat club colour of the school's Christ Church college, which the majority of the crew attend). It is unclear why the Cambridge crew accessorize their whites with a pink/scarlet sash.

For their 1836 match, crew colours for both schools remain the same, however Cambridge includes a light-blue ribbon (at the request of some of its crew to honour *their* college, Gonville & Caius, and its boat club colour) on the bow of their boat. Cambridge wins by twenty lengths.

The light blue of the ribbon—Cambridge blue—is actually a shade of teal green.

Christmas, 1924. Raw winds scratch across the lake, crawl up the bluff to the Shoreview. Sleet bites at the windows. Best we stay inside, Gran says.

You at the kitchen table: eight-going-on-nine and hard at it, struggling with the dull stub of your well-chewed Dixon Classmate HB. You trace another sporting triumph as illustrated in your *Boy's Own* holiday number: the Cambridge Eight thumping Oxford by four and a half going away.

Grey lead residue and yellow shavings dirty your shirt sleeves from cuff to elbow; your tracing is a crime scene of black fingerprints.

Gran glances over your shoulder. A bit of blue, she says. My kingdom for a bit of blue.

Bess giggling under the table, clumsy fingers undoing your laces.

Your lines wander, the paper tears. JEEZBESSLEAVEOFF!

Bess dodges your glancing shoe; howls like her throat's been cut. Enough, Gran says.

You and Bess are bundled in your itchiest home knits and everyone's off to the downtown emporiums.

Faber-Castell, makers of artist materials since 1761, launches its Polychromos brand of coloured pencils in 1908. The pencils, praised for their vividness, sit easily in the hand by way of a round-barrelled design turned in cedar wood. Each colour core is oil-based, making them ideal for working in fine detail.

The basic twelve-colour box includes:
101: white
107: cadmium yellow
110: phthalo blue
115: dark cadmium orange
133: magenta
140: light ultramarine
162: light phthalo green
163: emerald green
177: walnut brown
187: burnt ochre
199: black
219: deep scarlet red

Gran buys a rag doll for Bess. For you a penknife that nestles in your palm as though made for no other.

These will need a sharpening, she says, handing you a narrow tin box. The italic swoop of *Polychromos* flows across the lid.

You pry open the box, revealing a beginner's dozen of colouring pencils. You whittle the twelve to fine points, leaving a rainbow crown of shavings on Bess's head.

You commit each pencil, colour and number, to memory.

You erase the most offending smudges and fingerprints, give your hands a scrubbing, set to reworking. Cambridge picks up the pace, bold strokes of 140 leaving Oxford's 110 crabbing in their wake.

Winter's jaws loosen, days grow longer; knits are folded and mothballed. Fresh breezes, open windows, clouds of midge-bugs form along the lake.

Come spring, the Shoreview uses its name to best advantage.

Years later, you will spend an evening pruning the overgrowth of notes and clippings and whatnot you've collected in an old textbook. Amid the amassed chaos, a blue report card you thought thrown away long ago. Dated in a teacher's hand: June 1926.

Reading/B        Comprehension good, shy to recite in class.
Penmanship/A    Excellent. Cursive work graceful.
History/C        Improving.
Geography/A      Lovely work, esp. maps. Uses colour well.
Arithmetic/F     Unsatisfactory. Consider home tutoring.
Art/B+           Lacks originality, yet industrious, exacting.
PhysTr/D         Poor. Reluctant to join in.

Only someone who had taught her share of the quiet and withdrawn would have saved such a thing; would have known that despite sitting unchosen in the gymnasium or silent in the back row, this distant fourth-grader could read and write, knew his north from south, so hang the times tables.

Only a grandmother would have kept such a report card, waiting for the right time to slip it in among your notes when you weren't looking.

By the 1920s the shoreline of Toronto's Sunnyside neighbourhood is one of the city's most popular escapes, averaging more than 300,000 visitors each summer.

The Sunnyside Amusement Park opens in 1922. Among other attractions, the park offers the Flyer roller coaster, the Derby Racer steeplechase ride, several carousels, and a variety of food concessions. There is a baseball stadium; one can hire a canoe by the hour. The Park is home to a variety of events, including flagpole sitting, beauty pageants, and diving horses. One can wager on the dog races, tap a toe in the dance hall, or eat their fill of Red Hots while strolling a boardwalk that hugs the lakeshore for almost three kilometres.

Next to the amusement park stands the Sunnyside Bathing Pavilion. The two wings of the beaux arts building contain outdoor changing areas, including lockers and showers (ladies to the right, gents to the left). A central staircase leads to an upper terrace stretching the length of the pristine white building, offering unobstructed views of the boardwalk, the beach, and the lake beyond.

But as Lake Ontario is deep and cold (and frustratingly slow to warm in the summer months), a swimming pool is opened beside the Pavilion in 1925. At the time, it is the largest outdoor pool in the world. Nicknamed "The Tank," it can hold two thousand bathers.

Thirteen, perhaps fourteen: You are standing knee-deep in the lake shallows, fists clenched, teeth chattering. You uncurl a finger, then another. One finger counts one step, two fingers two steps. Three to the drop-off and you'll be in over your head.

At the water's edge, Bess and current-best-friend-what's-her-name hardly conceal the snorts and guffaws, yell HEYCHICKENLEGS, start in with the barnyard noises. Gran shushes the girls and offers her lifeguard advice.

Mind where you wander, good prince.

*SergeantMajorHatesEatingOnions*: Superior, Michigan, Huron, Erie, Onions for Ontario, the last great lake in the line.

Great as may be, but stand in those shallows and Onions becomes an ocean sea: her thermoclines raising gooseflesh on your arms; draining the blush from your cheeks; cooling the heat of your sunburnt shins.

It is the summer your face erupts in spots; your joints develop clicks and grinds. By August, your voice wanders from squeaks to grunts, finally to settle an octave lower.

Gran backs you against the kitchen door frame. Tonguing her pencil, she balances it on the crown of your head, parts your mop of hair, scribes a line on the frame, then annotates: *H, 8/30*. Three inches in as many months.

There's corn in Egypt, she says.

Fourteen, then.

Which makes Bess *such* an annoyance and *such* a girl and *such* a nine-year-old—JEEZBESSQUITWITHTHESKINNY JOKES!

It is the summer you learn that corn in Egypt means good things have arrived and plenty of them. It is also the summer you learn that for all Bess's sauce and cheek, her revolving door of best friends, her uncanny ability to ignore consequences, her ceaseless pestering—JEEZHENRYDON'T BESUCHACLUCKCLUCK!—there is a part of you that wishes you could have as much fun in your own skin.

But one would never admit that to a kid sister.

As impossible as it is for you to visualize, shivering in those shallows, there will come a summer when that sister will wave your train away to Halifax, to a troopship, to a war. Standing on the station platform, wee Bess will become Elizabeth before your eyes.

You squint beyond the breakwater. A bulbous ship appears through the haze, stalls a passing gull. The bird backflaps in search of a landing.

You shade your eyes as the ship's lookout coils a rope around his forearm. He swings in a graceful arc from the crow's nest, ranting his way to the deck. Brothers, can you not smell them, can you not taste them; for all that is holy, can you not see them?

*Bienvenidos a las Indias.* Welcome to the Indies.

A modest carrack-style merchant ship, the *Santa María* carries Christopher Columbus on his first voyage from Spain to the Americas. She is accompanied by the caravels *Niña* and *Pinta*.

The *Santa María* is approximately twenty metres long with a beam of some six metres; she carries a crew of forty. Broad through the middle and not particularly agile, with a single deck and three short masts, she is in effect a cargo scow neither designed nor intended for exploration.

On Christmas Day, 1492, the *Santa María* runs aground off Hispaniola, her timbers salvaged to build an onshore garrison. Columbus departs the island three weeks later, returning to Spain aboard the *Niña*.

The fat little ship tacks for a shore the crew were certain would never appear. Have faith, the captain said as they shipped anchor in Palos, there is no end to it, no edge at all. Round the world is, as round as your fool heads, and by God and Isabella it is west that will bring us east.

The crew could only watch as Spain and home sank behind them.

*Océano mar*, said the empty half of the charts. The ocean sea.

Lining the starboard rail, the crew follows the lookout's finger. For all that is holy, brothers, is that not our *niño*? There, in the shallows, the shivering waif?

Weekenders fill the beach; they're three deep along the terrace of the bathing pavilion. Everyone busies themselves with anchoring blankets, setting out picnic lunches, bantering about the heat,

*positively lethal,*

the rise of those Nazis and their angry little man,

*there'll be the Devil to pay,*

the change room queues,

*we should write a letter,*

snaking as far as the Guess Your Weight booth,

*in no uncertain terms.*

The Spaniards appear every summer, bumping into a new world inhabited not by mandarins or maharajas but by complaining picnickers wiping ice cream from their chins, Gran pouring the sand out of her shoes, Bess and what's-her-name trying to distract the lifeguards.

Every summer as you watch the Spaniards furl sail, you raise an open palm. *Amigo.*

The gull folds its wings and settles in the rigging. The crew choke on the lumps in their throats. On your knees, brothers, and thank your God and Queen. Ask them by what holy miracle they have kept us safe.

Standing in the shallows, you would do anything to join the Spaniards. Theirs is a brotherhood that stands nose-to-nose against the schoolyard toughs; defies their hovering grandmothers; betters their kid sisters. A brotherhood risking it all: the black fathoms under their keel, the empty half of the charts, the third step.

You would learn how to swim: let the water close over your head, dog-paddle out beyond the breakwater. Muscle yourself to the deck, regulation pirate-issue cutlass clenched in your teeth.

Then again: a brother would not dog-paddle.

Ready?

You glance back to the beach. Gran offers a thumbs-up then reaches into her bag for a handful of coins, scattering them over your head and into the water.

Cheeks puffed, nose pinched, you squat until the water rises to your forehead. You squeeze your eyes closed, desperately groping along the drop-off. Feeling your way to a treasure that should be just out of reach.

Chest tightening, lungs screaming. You surface empty-handed, slapping at your face, sputtering back to shore. Gran stands ready with a towel.

Open your eyes, good prince. You'll find nothing in the dark.

The ocean sea: she cooled your sunburned knees, caressed your bony thighs; shrivelled your private bits-and-pieces. Her currents slid like silk between your fingers. When did the sea become a woman?

First year university, Comparative Literature: An Introduction; you fighting to stay awake through Homer. The Penelopiad, the Sirens, the works.

A month in, you drop the CompLit and bounce through alternatives: antiquities (more dull Greeks); philosophy (duller still); business (of all things). Nothing sticks. You reconsider bricklaying.

American realist painter N.C. Wyeth produced some three thousand works of art and illustrated over a hundred books, including Defoe's *Robinson Crusoe*, Lanier's *The Boy's King Arthur*, and Fenimore Cooper's *Last of the Mohicans*. His colour plates for Stevenson's *Treasure Island* are considered masterpieces of commercial illustration.

Wyeth's palette consisted of umbers, sepias, and ochres with occasional shades of blue, red, and vibrant yellow. His compositions were bold and graphic, his use of light as much drama as decoration: the principal character's face often obscured in shadow.

When illustrating a novel, Wyeth knew he was a collaborative storyteller. Rather than rendering scenes the author had already handled in detail, Wyeth chose briefer, passing moments—Stevenson's description of Jim leaving home is a succinct one sentence, yet Wyeth's painting of the scene is a treatise on character, mood, and emotion.

While illustration paid his bills and made him famous, Wyeth grew to loathe his dependence on commercial work, complaining that any creativity was being handcuffed by the technical demands of book printing.

Bricklaying, Gran says. Over my dead body.

She stands in your bedroom doorway, surveying the piles of *Boy's Own* tracings gathering dust under your bed, the doodle-filled primers heaped in a corner, the painstaking copies of Wyeth's knights and pirates and Crusoe and Friday and young Jim, the reminders of how you managed to transform what anyone might see into what only you could see. How the faces you coloured became eccentric, interesting; the settings you copied became exotic, inviting; the events you traced became adventures.

It is all abracadabra, Gran says. A few strokes of line and shade and hue and the ordinary becomes your extraordinary. How you magically appear at Stanley's elbow, holding his coat while he machetes his way to Livingstone. And isn't that you sitting cox in the Cambridge boat?

You gather an entrance portfolio for the Fine Arts department's admissions board.

In eighteenth-century Europe, the preferred model for training fine artists relied on the use of copying. Beginning students redrew engravings of famous paintings; progressed to sketching plaster casts of statues from antiquity; finally attempted a copy of the aforementioned painting itself. Having demonstrated suitable proficiency, students then moved on to life drawing.

Once the student became the artist, copying moved from repetition to translation: in essence saying the same thing but using a different language. To hone his talent as a draftsman, Edgar Degas painted a version of Poussin's *The Rape of the Sabine Women*. John Singer Sargent freely admitted to admiring, and referencing, various works by Velázquez.

The reclining nude of Giorgione's *Sleeping Venus* (1510) begat Titian's *Venus of Urbino* (1534) which in turn begat Manet's *Olympia* (1863). Each one at once a copy and an original.

The admissions board reviews your portfolio. They make it clear that while there appears to be a balanced palette, a grasp of composition, a naive awareness of styles and isms, and certainly an ability to copy, your work is just that. Meticulous but unoriginal.

You tack hard: Could your tracings be a start rather than a finish? Must your copying go further than *Boy's Own* heroics; should you be taking on history's masterpieces, studying their whens, dissecting their whys, absorbing their hows?

You gather your portfolio, turn to leave. The faculty dean calls you back. Ever thought about art history, young man?

In 1919 art historian Helen Gardner becomes head of the photography and lantern slide department at the Art Institute of Chicago's Ryerson Library. She begins teaching there the following year. Frustrated by the lack of a comprehensive art history text, she writes one herself.

*Art through the Ages* is first published in 1926. At the time it is the only single-volume work covering art's international history. The book's scope is exhaustive, extending from the paleolithic to the twentieth century, surveying not only western Europe's canon but also India, the Far East, and Indigenous America. The text quickly becomes requisite, rising to the top of a student's reading list.

Subsequent editions will be published as *Gardner's Art through the Ages*. Inevitably, the academic community will shorthand the title, as in "Where are we in Gardner, class?"

New students in art history are advised to acquaint themselves with Gardner: her *Art through the Ages* is considered the
definitive text. At your entry interview, the registrar looks up
from your CV and suggests you would be wise to follow such
counsel.

The bank of Gran advances the funds to buy a copy.

Addenda begin filling your Gardner's margins. Not a page goes unmarked by your underlining paragraphs or circling words. You slip in pieces clipped from newspapers and magazines; insert obscure minutiae copied on everything from matchbook covers to napkins. There are blurred monochromes and garish plates scissored from other texts; drafts of rash opinions and unsubstantiated theories; re-created colour wheels, spectrums, optic diagrams. You recount, you diarize, numbering your entries without much order, even less index.

You long to visit the world's grand museums: the Louvre, the Prado. In the meantime you haunt the Art Gallery of Toronto. A little less grand perhaps; for a boy from Sunnyside, certainly no Uffizi. You sketch, copy, annotate your Canadians: Krieghoff's *habitants*, Kane's noble tribes, Jackson's landscapes.

Your first note, in much-practised cursive: an encyclopedia entry re the connection between volcanoes in the South Pacific and the skies in a Turner landscape. You slip the note somewhere among the Romantics.

Gran also bankrolls the purchase of a traveller's paintbox: an elaborate wooden affair, brass handled and hinged, the size of a small suitcase.

Inside are compartments for various brushes, graphite sticks, and chalks; a cut-crystal water dish, hidden drawers for sharpeners and erasers. Nestled under the lid, a ream of thick watercolour paper.

Ceramic trays hold small cakes of colour, though not the numbered primaries of your coloured pencils. These morsels are Colour: titled, capitalized, transformed.

Red is no longer your 219 nor yellow your 107. Time to consider Sienna, Vermilion, Alizarin. To think Lemon, Cadmium, Gamboge.

Options become endless. Green could be Veronese, Viridian, Terre Verte. Blue might be Egyptian, Cobalt, Prussian; browns in Umber, Fallow, Van Dyke. Charcoal or Lamp or Ink instead of black; white could be Chinese or Lead or Titanium.

None of Gran's *RichardOfYorkGaveBattleInVain* here.

You tick the proper boxes: cum laude in art history (a year early); Grand Tour graduate studies (Paris some, detours to Amsterdam and Provence, Rome and Florence mostly); the appointment (senior lecturer). Check check check.

You abandon a moustache that refuses to fill in. Replace with wire-framed spectacles. Tortoiseshell, the optometrist says, a studious choice, sir.

By then Gardner's case boards are warping under the bulk of accumulated miscellany. Gran begins calling it your pillow book.

You decide the department can do without its cracked, over-exposed lantern slides. Instead, you copy the syllabus paintings onto any surface you can find.

For want of canvas you stretch tablecloths and bedsheets—
Gran donates her guest linens. From the History department
come liberated classroom maps: *Political Divisions of the Indian
Subcontinent (Railways Shown Thus)*; *The United States including
the Westward Movement of Population to 1870*.

It all becomes a production:
   remove maps from poles,
   unroll same, blank side up,
   weight corners, smooth creases,
   rule grid over reference outlines,
   transfer said grid,
   then said outlines,
   to said blank side;
   take up the brush.

In time Brueghel's peasants play their games, Lucretia bleeds
for Rembrandt; Monet's Giverny grows more verdant.

To patrons of the 1819 Paris Salon, Théodore Géricault's painting *Scène de naufrage* (Shipwreck scene) appears all too familiar. Not surprising: the painting depicts the aftermath of the headline-making wreck of the French frigate *Méduse* three years earlier.

Poor navigation and suspect seamanship caused the *Méduse* to run aground off the coast of Mauritania. One hundred and forty-seven sailors and civilians were then cast adrift on a hastily constructed raft. Only fifteen survived to be rescued two weeks later, having endured starvation, murder, and cannibalism. (Géricault chooses to paint the moment when the fifteen, huddled on the ruins of the slowly sinking raft, realize that a ship—and potential rescue—has appeared on the far horizon.)

The disaster caused an international scandal, due in no small measure to the incompetence of the ship's captain and the subsequent lack of effort by French authorities to rescue anyone.

Géricault's painting is massive, bleak, and dark; in places virtually black; the palette thick with brown and umber, particularly in the skies threatening the central composition of *Méduse* castaways. These desperate figures form a pyramid of shadow and light, pallid whites and deathly greys, all surrounded by an ocean thick in muddy greens. If there is any hope in this scene, it is in the streak of sunlight along the horizon, illuminating a very small, very distant sail.

The painting becomes known as *The Raft of the Medusa*.

To the back of *Prevailing Currents of the Equatorial Oceans* you spend a term rushing a forgery of Géricault's *Scène*. You go through a gallon of brown house paint (the man at the hardware store cocks a wary eyebrow when you ask for umber) that you further darken with a gallon of black. It takes you a week just to blend a suitably seasick green. When you step back to assess your finished work, you realize you've skewed the perspective, located the horizon too low, left out a castaway altogether.

You decide the result is passable, if only for the irony. Would that the *Méduse* had had such a map.

Open your eyes, good prince. You'll find nothing in the dark.

A hallway; your hand blindly reaching through a doorway to find a light switch. A yellow glow slowly fills the lecture theatre; students shuffle past. You survey the hallway for stragglers.

You walk to the lectern, arrange your notes. April 1940, end of term. A dozen faces today, not the worst showing, considering. You clear your throat.

Where were we?

Copies of Gardner appear from shoulder bags, dead weights thumping onto desks. The eager flip through notebooks, the bored slump and fidget. Give or take a year or two, a degree or two, you aren't much older than they are.

Anyone?

Front row centre, she jabs a manicured finger at her notebook. The Baroque, sir.

Dear Alice.

You feel your cheeks flush, ears burn. You turn your back to the class and unroll the day's lesson, *Conversion on the Way to Damascus.* The voice in your head suggests that you show some backbone jesus man don't meet her eye fuck fuck fuck *fuck* anyone but Alice.

You turn to face the class, take a breath.

Right, yes ... the Baroque ... Rome, then ... the church of Santa Maria del Popolo.

You can't seem to focus, you resort to shorthand:
Saul of Tarsus,
road to Damascus,
burst of holy light,
spooked horse,
Saul on his backside,
hapless servant holding the reins,
voice of God,
Saul reaching for heaven,
divine light blinding,
three days pass,
Saul becomes the all-too-visionary Paul.

1593. Fillide Melandroni, aged twelve, moves to Rome. Her mother puts her to work as a prostitute. Fillide rises to become a favourite courtesan of the wealthy and connected, including those Vatican nabobs inclined toward intimate female companionship. One of her clients, the banker and impresario Vincenzo Giustiniani, flaunting his taste in both art and women, commissions her portrait. The artist is the ambitious miscreant Caravaggio, the painting *Portrait of a Courtesan*.

On the surface the portrait may be a banker's ideal of physical beauty, yet it is the ugliness of Roman street life that underpaints Fillide's expressions, her body language, her attitude. She is the physical embodiment of Caravaggio's desire to bring a warts-and-all humanity to his renderings of the biblical epic. As such, he casts Fillide in other roles: a defiant Saint Catherine, a sceptical Mary Magdalene, or most notably a merciless Judith, scowling through her decapitation of an Assyrian general as though she were dispatching a reluctant chicken.

Fillide dies in 1618. In spite of her years of "service" to various officials of the Vatican, the Church denies her a Christian burial.

Alice follows your fingers as they outline the *Conversion*'s chiaroscuro, your hands stroking the horse's lowered head; your outstretched arms echoing Saul/Paul's heavenward reach. The more you flap and flail, the closer in she leans.

You realize you are rambling: how the servant and his kind are recurring features in Caravaggio's work; that the streetwalkers, layabouts, and urchins he employed as models—a blind pilgrim and his servant on the road to Damascus, a dubious Thomas probing the wounds of Christ, a frowning Judith beheading Holofernes—on any other day are the artist's neighbours.

So, you say, a whore will play Caravaggio's Virgin, a gutter drunk will stand in as his Saint Matthew. The artist will go so far as to sever his own head to portray David's vanquished Goliath. Any theories as to why?

In the front row, up goes a hand.

Alice, naturally.

Black (a dominant genetic trait) is the most common hair colour in the world, containing large amounts of eumelanin polymers. The generic term *black* as it relates to hair can be described as raven, jet, ink, pitch, or obsidian (named for a deep-black volcanic glass created when lava, rich in feldspar and quartz, rapidly cools).

Egypt's Fourth Dynasty recipe for manufacturing blue (known chemically as calcium copper silicate) involved firing then grinding then re-firing a mix of limestone, malachite, and sand. The resulting "Egyptian blue"—a close match to nature's turquoise and lapis lazuli—was highly valued, representing the desert sky, the river Nile, and the deity Amun-Ra, itself often depicted with blue skin.

Her hair, then: layered strokes of obsidian, neatly parted, a lazy curl descending to one ear. It's called a bob, Bess says, quite the fashion, well done you.

Her eyes: Egyptian blue, flecked with green, sloping to the outside corners. A crooked tooth catches her lip when she smiles—often and unnervingly in your direction.

Her voice: a cocktail of mezzo-soprano and cigarette smoke.

Leaving the lecture theatre, she slips you a note saying she might be found over the summer dressing windows at a downtown emporium. Were one so inclined, sir.

Discreet as ever, Alice.

Come June you are tapping on an emporium window with one hand, the other holding a bouquet of yellow (gamboge, to be precise) gardenias. Inside, Alice charades *movie?*

You settle on the Revue, a late showing of *That Hamilton Woman*. Afterwards you walk her home, share a smoke; risk a kiss. She stops you with a hand against your chest, slips a lozenge between her teeth.

Now, she says.

Her lips: softer and wetter than even you could have thought possible. And like her nail polish: vermilion, oh so vermilion.

She pulls away, leaving a peppermint whisper of isn't-that-Vivien-Leigh-an-enchantress lingering in your ear.

Tea. With. Gran.

Not your idea, though Gran (who *suggests* you do the inviting) then Alice (who *suggests* it might be overdue) make it feel like it is. Consensus settles on a Sunday afternoon.

You and Alice arrive at the Shoreview. Your palms are damp, your mind conjuring Holmes v. Moriarty, Elizabeth the First v. Mary the Scot, chalk v. cheese. As you climb the stairs to Gran's flat, it occurs to you that your worry isn't that these women might be too different; rather they might be too much alike.

You warn Alice that Gran may have questions.

Parents? Alice says. Lovely people, ma'am. Father's a captain of industry, mother's a player of bridge, arranger of luncheons, writer of charity cheques. Siblings? One tiresome brother who believes families like ours own the emporiums, they do not work in them.

Schooling? Honour roll throughout, thanks to a string of diligent tutors and nannies. University not optional, household sciences strongly advised. Humanities gave everyone a fit, father stopped covering tuition, mother still waiting for the phase to end. Been paying my way ever since.

Cards, ma'am? As in poker? Never played.

Love life? With respect, ma'am, I'm not sure it's anyone's business, but yes, a few boys. Nothing serious, each a thinner version of his own captain-of-industry father. Each as vapid as the one before. Let's just say we've all made errors in judgment. But along comes your grandson and here we are.

Imagine the luck.

For you, the afternoon consists of equal parts bystander, bartender, busboy. Awkward silences are few and deftly overcome; verbal missteps fewer still. Even your ignorance re Gran's preferred flowers proves inconsequential. At the florist, Alice had waved you off the roses—*could we at least try to be less predictable*—choosing instead a handful of day lilies.

After Gran's initial interrogation, the visit loosens up. There's a lively conversation regarding Shakespeare's only Irish character (*Henry V*'s Macmorris); a brief review of trends in window display (hemlines creeping up the calf, an unfortunate reliance on shoddy mechanics and awkward puppetry); a hand or two of One-Eyed Jacks; and a few fingers of Tullamore Dew, Alice revealing an unexpected inability to hold her whiskey.

Your first night together. Alice turns off the lights. You won't be needing those spectacles, professor.

Your eyes adjusting to the darkness, she straddles your hips. You stare at her blurred outlines, searching for shades, highlights, detail.

Marry me, Alice.

The two of you mug for the camera, leaning against a coin-operated sightseeing binocular machine. The image is out-of-focus, happy couple off-centre, perpetual cloud of Niagara mist looming behind. On the back of the photograph, in Alice's hand: *July '41, honeymooners!*

The thought of a church wedding had knotted your stomach: the guests, the display, the ceremony of it all. Your future mother-in-law pressed for the grandest of nuptials, the society event of the season. But there was a war on; thankfully, Alice played the decorum card. She too had no wish to be the centre of attention. That said, she said she would be dressing up: pillbox hat, fishnet veil, the appeasement of her mother's pearls.

You marry at city hall, one more nervous couple in a queue of dozens, the proceedings brief and by the book. Alice looks fantastic in shades of cream. You feel funereal in suit and waistcoat. The clerk obligingly witnesses, then holds your wife's bouquet while she co-signs the paperwork.

On the road to Niagara Falls (a friend of Alice's loans you the car), all you can do is laugh. My *wife*, you keep repeating. In a Ford *De Luxe*, Alice says.

Until then you might have held Alice's hand more by accident than intent, managed a discreet embrace or peck on the cheek once in a while. On the cruise under the falls, you throw propriety to the mist. You embrace Alice, lean her back against the boat's railing. The other passengers move aside. Soaked through, you kiss her like Nelson leaving for Trafalgar. You both acknowledge the crowd's applause: a bow, a curtsey, a wave.

Strolling the esplanade, you feed Alice ice cream. The tourist photographer (dollar a picture, three-for-two) suggests you both stand next to the binocular machine. The mugging is your idea.

It is the last time you remember not having a worry in the world.

Vienna, 1911. Walburga (Wally) Neuzil meets expressionist Egon Schiele then spends the next few years as the artist's lover and inspiration. While these years are among Schiele's most productive—his *Portrait of Wally* is considered one of his most striking works—he marries another woman in 1915, then cryptically suggests that Wally, the new wife, and himself might enjoy a "triangular" relationship. The refusal of the two women is, not surprisingly, unequivocal.

Meanwhile, fourteen-year-old Alice Prin begins posing nude for the artists of Paris. She eventually becomes one of the most sought-after models in the city, enjoys success as actress and chanteuse, changes her name to Kiki de Montparnasse. In 1924 the American artist Man Ray makes her an icon of Surrealism, photographing her as *Le Violon d'Ingres*, her naked spine bracketed with two f-holes.

The wife of polymath artist William Morris, the intelligent, independent Jane Morris becomes muse (and rumoured paramour) to her husband's contemporary Dante Gabriel Rossetti. As a founding member of the Victorian Pre-Raphaelites, Rossetti considers her beauty to be the very embodiment of the movement. So besotted is he that he paints her as the Roman goddess Proserpine in not one but eight different versions, *and* writes a sonnet to her name.

Home from the Falls. Alice hovers over your preparations for the coming term. On your easel: the grid-lined beginnings of Rossetti's first rendition of his *Proserpine*.

You manage Rossetti's adjectives: the curving grace of the goddess's hands, her gentle grasp of the opened pomegranate. The shimmer of blue folds in her garment, the flawless olive warmth of her skin; the dark, hooded eyes, the demure downward glance.

You finish with the waves of Proserpine's dark mane of hair. And her bee-stung lips: a crimson echo of the fruit she holds in her hand.

You step back to clean your brushes, ask Alice her opinion.

Honestly? It's all a bit *male*. Flawless, I suppose, but so idealized, so expected. So, well, *fake*. You're not going to write me a poem, are you?

Struggling to find an aesthetic that would visualize his concepts of personal identity, the sculptor and painter Amedeo Modigliani looks for inspiration not only among his Paris contemporaries—Picasso, Brancusi, and the like—but farther afield than the studios of Montmartre and Montparnasse.

It is in the city's Musée d'ethnographie du Trocadéro—founded in 1878 to satisfy the public's fascination with the plunder from various French colonial adventures—that Modigliani studies the Indigenous masks, sculptures, and other artifacts taken from Africa, the Far East, and the South Pacific.

Through these "spoils" he develops his unique approach to portraiture. Elongated faces, stretched bodies, pupilless eyes, miniature mouths will come to define his legacy. His work is considered by some a banal collection of graphic abstracts, depersonalized, the subjects monotonously similar. Yet it is in his command of subtle detail—the tilt of a head, the arc of a neck, the pose of the hands, the richness of palette—that his portraits become a gallery of individuals.

Alice picks up your Gardner, consults the index, turns to twentieth-century Europe. Try her, she says. The book falls open to Modigliani's portrait of Fernande Barrey.

Mme Barrey is stretched bone-thin, her arms discreetly covered, crossed at the lap. Her shapeless black dress betrays little allure; her swanlike neck is unadorned. Her hair (colour matching her dress) is bobbed, fringed, nondescript save a slight curl across her cheek.

You copy Modigliani's portrait-as-mask with care, the woman's ovoid eyes more enigmatic than lifeless. You finish with a small dab of vermilion lip.

Now, Alice says, is this portrait closer to reality? Plain to some, dull even, but I'd wager the practical hair, the modest dress, and the hidden physique are nearer the truth than any man's lovestruck notion of goddess. Though I'm not sure I share Mme Barrey's eyes.

The gimmick of creating extravagant window displays to attract holiday customers begins with Macy's department store in New York City in 1874. By the turn of the century, the practice grows to include everything from mechanical reindeer to hydraulic lifts to live actors as Santas-and-elves, and spreads across North America to the emporiums of Europe and the UK.

The most ambitious windows in Canada are at Eaton's flagship store in Toronto and, directly across the street, at its rival emporium Simpson's. Weekend shoppers flocking to see the competing windows, crowds spilling off the sidewalks (walking from Eaton's to Simpson's requires using what is known as the "cattle crossing"), make for a death-defying mix of pedestrians and automobiles, particularly on Saturdays. (In the then pious Toronto, stores are closed on Sundays. Eaton's takes its piety seriously, using curtains to obscure its holiday windows.)

13 December 1941, a Saturday. Freezing drizzle glazes the city. Alice steps into the street to avoid a herd of gawking pedestrians. A passing driver stands on his useless brakes as his truck slides over her.

The police arrive at your flat. You forget your manners—the constable's mouth is moving, but you seem to have gone momentarily deaf. You invite the man to step in out of the weather, catch the word *wife*.

Not here right now ... went to see the Christmas windows ...

Is there a problem, constable?

You blame the driver,
the weather,
the crowds,
the emporium windows, the machine-stiff Saint Nick, the papier-mâché reindeer hanging over a lopsided barber pole stuck in a snowbank of cotton batting.

You blame the Japanese air force for bombing Pearl Harbor the week before, for pushing America into the war, for forcing the New York museum to cancel your guest fellowship, for costing you the hefty rental deposit on a walk-up in the East Village, for denying Alice a visit to Macy's and its famous windows.

You blame the you who should have sensed Alice's disappointment, who should have put aside grading essays on a Saturday, who would have followed her as she bounced out the door with the energy of a four-year-old.

Should have, would have.

You struggle with what might be worse: lying dead in the street for the sake of a Christmas display or enduring the clichéd melodrama of the grieving spouse—the empty bottles, the paralyzing hangovers, the missed lectures, missed meals, missed days. The pounding fists bleeding across a smashed mirror.

You cry out in the night, sheets drenched, certain she is standing at the foot of the bed. You fumble for your spectacles in the bottomless dark. No shading, no highlights, no details.

Édouard Manet paints his *Le Suicidé* sometime between 1877 and 1881. Considered by some an anomaly amid his more famous works, the painting depicts a young man collapsed across a bed, mouth agape, apparently having just shot himself (his limp hand still holds the gun). A scarlet smear spreads over the victim's torso.

Rejecting the tradition of depicting such tragedy as historical event or noble sacrifice or heroic gesture (Jacques-Louis David's *The Death of Socrates* comes to mind), Manet offers no grand gesture with *Le Suicidé*. There is no sense of specific time or place, no obvious explanation for what has just happened. The painting is raw, unadorned, the setting ordinary.

Even the dead man is anonymous.

Thoughts of ending it all rise like bile in your throat.

Art, once your trusted counsel, offers no direction. No scene to copy, no exit-by-example, no escape. You briefly consider Manet's *Le Suicidé* then remind yourself that you have neither the courage nor the pistol to pull it off.

Bess arrives to fuss and vacuum and bake things. She keeps mentioning how sad it is that you've lost her. You know she means well, though she might remember that Alice was not the family pet.

You leave your flat, bump against passersby; silently curse their oblivious if apologetic disregard.

Time flatlines: you lose wheres-and-whens; any structure to your days goes soft, unsteady. You arrive too early or too late, assuming you recall the commitment at all. Gone is any sense of anticipation or urgency: you couldn't care less if your students paid any attention or even showed up; if Gran planned to serve Sunday roast or Friday fish; if the weather along the beach deserved the walk.

A sleepless, starless, moonless night by the lake, heat oppressive, Alice gone months now. You are walking past the Sunnyside pavilion, staring out at a still and empty ocean sea.

Alice rushes past, a naked blur knocking you sideways, hair flying, laughter echoing off the pavilion. She hits the water at a run, three strides and under she dives. You follow the trail of bubbles; she breaks the surface. Smiling *that* smile, a curled finger beckons.

Off with the trousers, professor. Let's see that dog-paddle.

For better or worse, for as long as you both etc., what remains will be the moments you and Alice shared. Your idyllic attempts at her portrait, her insisting on a greater originality.

Less Rossetti, more Modigliani, professor.

The artist and illustrator Pierre Bonnard, a leading figure in the transition from French impressionism to modernism, is known for his intense colour palette (applied with meticulous small brushwork) and complex compositions. Influenced by the graphic arts of Japan, he paints landscapes, urban street views, and intimate domestic scenes populated with family and friends. The first portrait he produces is that of his future wife, Marthe.

Bonnard's preference for painting banal everyday life—particularly his own—leads some critics to call him an "Intimist," and over several decades Marthe becomes his constant model and beloved muse. He photographs her naked, as reference for lighting and pose. He paints her at their kitchen table, or unabashedly nude, or in a series of portraits of her reclining in the bath.

She becomes ageless, immortal. He paints her as a young woman, in her middle years, and well after her death.

You and Alice carry on conversations. Anticipating her birthday, she reminds you of favourite things: food (cream ices), book (*Little Women*), perfume (Guerlain's Shalimar). You tell her of your day; ask if she managed to finish the fall windows, remind her that you have papers to mark over the weekend; did she remember to check the mailbox? You mention that Gran expects us for a visit, more you than we actually, and no we aren't to bring anything.

Alice offers an opinion regarding your latest copying effort. I thought you hated Bonnard, she says.

The memories, the conversations, the thought of Bonnard persevering; grief becoming an ache not to be overcome, but to be managed. Chronic, endurable.

As though you have any other choice.

During the Second World War, propaganda broadsheets feature any number of inspirational messages, from the heartfelt to the racist. Among the most popular themes:

Rally-Round-the-Flag. To wit: fill the enlistment centres, invigorate morale. Phrases like *Lick Them Over There!* or *Let's Go Canada!* caption images of adventurous young men posed in freshly pressed uniforms, ready-aye-ready for the fight.

Defend-the-Home-Front. Overseas duty gives way to protecting hearth and family. Slogans like *Keep This Horror from Your Home* invariably frame a huddled group of women and children. Looming over this frightened (read defenceless) tableau: a clawed hand or bloodied weapon or hackneyed (as in drooling through bared teeth) portrait of the enemy.

Keep-Up-the-Fight. Enter the Victory Bond approach of *You Serve by Saving* or *Help Finish the Job*. The idealized fighting man is replaced by the grit of the weary veteran. Put plainly: War is no adventure, it is a fight for survival, and someone is actually putting their life on the line. The least the home front can do is open its wallet.

Fall, 1942. You hardly notice the change in weather. The morning editions compete for readers with their arrow-filled battle maps and endless casualty lists and dire analyses; telephone poles and hoarding boards are covered with relentless punctuation: *Your Chums Are Fighting, Why Aren't You? They Menace Canada on Both Coasts! You've Got a Date with a ~~Blonde~~ Bond!*

Gran plays her inevitable Shakespeare trump: when the blast of war blows in our ears then imitate the action of the tiger.

Point taken: you stiffen the sinews and summon up the blood.

Acoustic startle reflex (ASR), an involuntary physical defence mechanism originating in the brain stem, occurs when the body senses imminent danger, in this case an auditory attack. The limbs tense, shoulders hunch, eyes close.

The severity of ASR can reflect a person's state of mind when they hear a loud noise (anything over 80 decibels). Someone under extreme stress might experience debilitating ASR, while a calm and composed individual would show no reaction at all. The calmer the person, the milder the reflex.

Depending on the calibre, a gunshot can produce 150 decibels.

In the recruiting office Alice hovers at your shoulder, smiles at the nice young man filling in the form, bats a mascaraed eyelash, flirts away your mistake.

An art teacher is not the kind of man you want, lieutenant. Bit of a nervous Nellie, even his sister beats on him. Very sorry to have wasted your time, aren't we, Henry?

Tell the man we're sorry.

Basic training; Alice knows why your hands shake. Why you shut your eyes on the rifle range, fire wild and blind, send everyone scrambling for cover.

Cause and effect, she informs the drill instructor. Tell him to squeeze the trigger and suddenly it's all bang-crash-and-flop-sweat: the explosion against his eardrum, the punch against his shoulder, the violent thud of the bullet hitting the hay bale (in his case missing altogether), the lethal hole left well off the mark. The whole business puts his nerves on edge. He'd be so much better behind a desk; wouldn't you agree, sergeant?

Sitting on your bunk, Alice reminds your barrack mates to listen to themselves, repeats their words back at them. You couldn't hit water, old man, if you fell out of the fekkin boat.

The army, as enthusiastic as the broadsheets, keeps you anyway. *Carry your weight! Take your mind off things! Bully for you!*

You and Bess and Gran find a quiet corner of the station, away from the crowd of departing soldiers and farewell entourages. A tearful Bess confesses her fear that you won't be coming home. Gran reminds her that her brother is tougher than he looks, that if he can survive the loss of a loved one, he can survive anything. She ought to know.

With that, you board a train to Halifax, to a troopship, to the war.

In the pre-dawn hours of 10 July 1943, British and Canadian forces land near the village of Pachino, Sicily. Onshore Italian batteries put up a feeble, outmatched resistance, eventually preferring surrender to suicidal battle. By sundown the Allies have secured beachheads and are moving inland. The residents of Pachino greet them as liberators.

Canadian officer B.G. Parker records the day in his diary: "The fun really started for me about 0300 hours. Terrific bombardment by our heavy guns. Not much firing seen on shore. Tricky loading landing craft because of heavy swell. Landed wetshod at 0645 hours. Surprise achieved. Saw about 60 prisoners; prisoners and civilians not very perturbed. Dug in north of the salt lakes. Hot as hell. Very heavy firing about 1600 hours. I move up to C company position, where we come under mortar and artillery fire. See our heavy mortars, self-propelled guns, which silence the enemy. We move off to Phase III."

Shoulder-to-shoulder on the heaving landing craft, you struggle to find your footing in the spray and the vomit; finally jumping clear and bracing for a footfall that doesn't come. Boots and packs and bandoliers fill with the Mediterranean, pulling everyone under.

Salt water burns your throat; your legs stretch to reach a bottom that should have been just off the end of the ramp.

Barely to your waist, the officers had said.

In his account of the Battle of Marathon, historian Herodotus describes an Athenian soldier being suddenly struck blind after watching a comrade die on the battlefield. The blindness lasts for years.

During the Seven Years War, Austrian physician Josef Leopold Auenbrugger studies soldiers recently returned from the fighting. He finds many to be withdrawn, nervous, and aloof. "Full of sighs and moans," he writes.

Veterans of the American Civil War complain of an affliction known as "soldier's heart"—a thumping in the chest, a shortness of breath, sometimes both. Henry Fleming, Union soldier and protagonist of *The Red Badge of Courage*, describes his own experiences as the "black weight of his woe."

During the First World War, the preferred term is "shell shock," initially thought to be caused by standing too close to exploding artillery. (Had this been an accurate theory, 40 percent of the casualties at the Somme—those with little or no visible wounds—would have remained unscathed by simply stepping back a few paces.)

In the Second World War, one in four American casualties suffer from "combat stress"—often characterized by a so-called thousand-yard stare. Meanwhile, British and Canadian army doctors use the term "battle fatigue."

Regardless of terminology, the psychological effects of war can appear (from a long list of possible symptoms) as flashbacks, nightmares, or hallucinations. These play no favourites, respect no rank. And no amount of training can prevent a battle-weary soldier from seeing things that are not there, reliving events that never happened, or hearing voices that speak only to him.

You remember wading to the beach, pouring the sea from your boots, heading inland. From there, Sicily becomes a tempest: a hillside olive grove silhouetted black and dead and twisting across a bleached sky; a midnight climb, hot and blind and terrified, to a hilltop village; a sniper-trap piazza, a screaming firefight, a blurred figure running scared.

In the whirlwind, you close your eyes and listen for Alice.

Following a winter of crippling anxiety, a falling-out with friend and colleague Paul Gauguin, and the mutilation of his own ear, Vincent van Gogh admits himself to the asylum of Saint-Paul de Mausole in Saint-Rémy. It is the spring of 1889.

Officially diagnosed with epilepsy, and despite occasional relapses into paranoia, Van Gogh's mental health improves. Confined to his room, he paints only the view from his window (minus the metal bars)—the trees and flowers of the asylum's garden. In time he moves *en plein air*, painting the characteristic landscapes of southeast France.

Over the following year Van Gogh will produce some 150 canvases (including his masterpiece, *The Starry Night*), at least fifteen of which feature groves of ancient, gnarled olive trees.

Writing to his brother Theo, Van Gogh describes the challenge of painting these groves. "The effect of daylight and the sky means there are endless subjects to be found in olive trees. For myself I look for the contrasting effects in the foliage, which changes with the tones of the sky. At times, when the tree bares its pale blossoms and big blue flies, emerald fruit beetles and cicadas in great numbers fly about, everything is immersed in pure blue. Then, as the bronzer foliage takes on more mature tones, the sky is radiant and streaked with green and orange, and then again, further into autumn, the leaves take on violet tones something of the colour of a ripe fig, and this violet effect manifests itself most fully with the contrast of the large, whitening sun within its pale halo of light lemon. Sometimes, too, after a shower I've seen the whole sky pink and orange, which gave an exquisite value and colouring to the silvery grey-greens. And among all this were women, also pink, who were gathering the fruit."

You are running through a hillside olive grove, chasing flailing shadows of yourself. The ground tilts, your feet slip on a path of yellow bricks. The grove spins into a stand of bullying apple trees, harassing your every step.

Suddenly you and Alice are in the back rows of the Revue: still showing *The Wizard of Oz* two years on, matinees only, come on in we're air-conditioned.

Exposed roots, hollows choked with deadfall. The sun pulls the sweat through your shirt. You double over, drop to your knees. Your head fills with mush; feverish chills crawl across your skin.

You stagger from the grove, limp into Dorothy's poppy field. It begins to snow; Emerald City appears over the next hill.

For the 1939 Hollywood interpretation of L. Frank Baum's novel *The Wonderful Wizard of Oz*, Dorothy's adventures in the Land of Oz—conceived by the producers as more a dream sequence than a classic tale of fantasy—are filmed in three-strip (red, green, blue) Technicolor.

The movie's first-act scenes in Kansas, its opening and closing credits, as well as Auntie Em's apparition in the Wicked Witch's crystal ball, are filmed in black-and-white then tinted in warm sepia tones.

Your last meal was a congealed mystery in a ration tin: your insides are seizing with hunger. Amid the dead olive trees, you claw for the witch's apples, scratching at the parched ground, fingernails splitting, knuckles bleeding. Your skull throbs, pushing your eyeballs out of their sockets.

How many days hiding? How many nights running?

To make the most of the Technicolor process, the cinematic palettes of *The Wizard of Oz*—the blues of Dorothy's gingham dress, the green skin of the Wicked Witch, the morphing hues of the Horse of a Different Colour, etc.—require intense lighting. Numerous arc lamps are used, often raising sound stage temperatures to over 100 degrees F. Combine the stifling heat with costumes, effects, and sets; the choreography of large ensembles of performers; the often eighteen-hour shooting days. Fainting among cast and crew becomes a common occurrence.

Technicolor also gives the producers licence to change various details from the source material. In Baum's novel, the Hollywood ruby of Dorothy's slippers is actually silver.

You and Alice watch as a sepia farmhouse, caught in a sepia twister, spins and lands with a bounce. Sepia Dorothy, in sepia gingham, opens her sepia door. The camera dollies over her shoulder and through the door; pans to reveal the Technicolor burst of Munchkinland.

Alice gasps like a schoolgirl, spills her popcorn in your lap.

Alice knows. She finds you on your knees among the olive trees, helps you to your feet, teases about the smell of what's left of your uniform. She pulls a perfumed handkerchief from her sleeve, cleans the sweat off your spectacles, holds your elbow as you steady yourself.

Alice knows what happened in the village.

You wipe the dust caked in the corners of your mouth, ask for a kiss. She puts a hand to your chest. Perhaps a shave first, professor.

Sorry, you say.

Hush now, Alice whispers. You couldn't have seen that girl any more than I could've seen the truck.

You stutter, grope, try to explain.

We ... crawling through a ravine ... pitch-black, hands and knees, blind as bats, no stars, no moon ... sun-up ... entered the village, hiding in doorways, running over bodies ... hot as hell ... stumbled into a piazza ... everything slows down ... speeds up ... so fast, too fast ... ears ringing ... the mortars, the smoke, the dust, the scream ...

FORFUCK'SSAKEPRIVATESHOOTSOMETHING.

The girl ... came out of nowhere ...

Alice nods, smiles as you finish, asks about the Christmas windows.

Your best ever, you say.

Should have seen what?

The sun's glare through mottled shade, black branches chafing in the wind, your knees hugged against your chest. Sweating, shivering, rough bark digging at your spine. You recall a Sunnyside hide-and-seek strategy: if you can't see Bess, she can't see you. You bury your face in your arms.

Heads up, soldier.

You work your eyes open, the lids sticky and pulling. You raise a trembling hand to block the light. Hovering silhouettes: two soldiers, matching MP-banded biceps, where-might-you-be-going smirks. A dusty boot gives your shins a nudge.

Should have seen what, private?

The provosts each take an arm, raise you to your feet.

What say we find you a bath.

734 BCE: On the east coast of Sicily, Greek colonists establish a settlement at Naxos. Exploring the area, they move north along the coast to a promontory, Monte Tauro, drawn to its dramatic cliffs, pristine beaches, and unobstructed vistas over the Mediterranean.

392 BCE: The city of Tauromenium (Taormina) is founded on the promontory. City fathers, making the most of the real estate, install the obligatory amphitheatre (in this instance featuring an unobstructed view of nearby Mount Etna). The city prospers as a vacation destination for the notables of Athens.

212 BCE: Taormina comes under the control of the Roman Empire. Patricians and consuls replace the Grecian elites; palatial holiday villas—stuccoed in saffron hues, creamy yellows, and rosy pinks—appear on the cliffsides. The original amphitheatre is renovated to become the second largest in Sicily. Some argue the view is improved.

## III

Morning light stretches across a weed-choked terrace. Cracked marble pavers, creepers run amok. Dawn warms the view over a rusted balustrade, down a precipice grown feral with palm and cactus, through a stand of umbrella pine to a wedge of beach, lapis water, and the silver lines of breaking waves.

You lean back, the steamer chair creaking for want of linseed and re-caning. Behind you, an apology for the furniture.

Hard on the ass, the voice says, but apparently there's a war on.

Dingy lab coat draped over rumpled uniform. Pocketed stethoscope, notebook under arm, captain's insignia on threadbare collar points. Frameless spectacles propped on close-cropped head, scruff of beard, tray balanced in one hand.

Then again, let us praise the Greeks for the view. Coffee?

He places the tray on a side table, arranges another chair, shares your gaze into the distance. A different time, a different place, a pressed wardrobe: he might have appeared as from thin air, asking who ordered the Campari.

The sun clears the balustrade; your new companion lights a cigarette.

The time has come, he says, to talk of many things.

Suddenly you and Bess are sitting transfixed at Gran's kitchen table. You are nine, maybe ten. Bess, at most five. Gran, mischief in her eyes, circles you both.

A loaf of bread, the Walrus said,
Is what we chiefly need:
Pepper and vinegar besides
Are very good indeed—
Now if you're ready, Oysters dear,
We can begin to feed.

You cover your ears, feigning your terror. Bess begs through her squeals. Please don't eat us, Mr. Walrus.

Your new companion exhales a series of smoke rings. Of shoes and ships and sealing wax, he says, and whether one can explain the whys and wherefores of a lost soldier and how he might have ended up here.

Pigs, you say.

Hmm?

And whether pigs have wings.

As you wish. As for the whys and wherefores, let us begin with the heres and nows. Welcome to the Villa Rossa.

Thomas Eakins, one of Victorian America's pre-eminent artists, specializes in portraits of leading figures in the arts, sciences, and medicine. Known for his realism, Eakins strives to capture a subject's unvarnished individuality, preferring to paint his subjects in their workaday environments.

Eakins's *The Gross Clinic* (1875) depicts Philadelphia surgeon and academic Samuel Gross—bloodied scalpel in hand—overseeing a procedure in a lecture theatre crowded with medical students. Huge in size, dense in population; Eakins labours for almost a year to complete the painting.

Faithful to the subject's profession is the rendering of both the sombre, dimly lit theatre and the attire of Dr. Gross and his team: ink-black formality from top to toe.

*The Gross Clinic* is a portrait of medicine as diligence, competence, scholarship. Yet at the time, the practice is as likely to be associated with miracle elixirs and quackery. A doctor's traditional tailoring, meant to reflect the seriousness and skill of the practitioner, more often inspires mistrust and fear, more undertaker than healer. At best a brocade waistcoat and pearl-pinned cravat might hide the grislier stains of the work.

Meanwhile, science, dressed as white-smocked laboratory researchers, is busy unravelling the mysteries of infection, the cause-and-care of disease, how the human body actually works. So too is the ministering nurse, busying herself in snowy uniform, dabbing an anxious brow (among more sordid tasks) or holding a clammy, terrified hand.

From alabaster to chalk, medical white comes to represent hygiene, health, hope.

Thus, fourteen years later, Eakins paints *The Agnew Clinic.* Again, the scene is a medical school operating theatre, this time with good Doctor Agnew conducting a partial mastectomy (and holding his own scalpel-as-baton). Setting and staging are familiar, but the house lights have come up, there's been a costume change. The theatre is bright to the point of glaring. Agnew and his assistants virtually glow in their white coats, aprons, and smocks.

And yet for all its advancements, medicine remains a dark art: an inscrutable practice that can make a patient feel uneasy, even threatened. The new wardrobe does little to help. Nerves still jitter, sweat still dampens the forehead, blood pressures still rise when one hears *the doctor will see you now.*

So much so that the medical profession coins a term: white coat syndrome.

The Red House, you say.

Indeed, Jack says. And so a bit of history: Said villa is built in the twenties by an expat baroness using her ex-husband's ex-fortune. The war starts, Jerry commandeers the place for an officers' mess, gives the lady of the house the heave-ho. Finally the Allies appear on the horizon, Jerry beats a hasty retreat, leaves the villa the worse for wear—exhibit A, your chair.

And the baroness?

Made your espresso this morning.

Is it captain or doctor?

I'm no more an officer than my dog, and the white coat just makes everybody nervous. My *nonna* calls me Giacomo. Jack will do.

Not a doctor, then.

Only of a sort. The army believes my particular field might be useful here. Insists on the medico coveralls. As for the uniform, they made me a captain because I happen to speak *la lingua*. Montreal Italian, mother's side. She insisted I learn the language of love.

I thought that was French.

Where I come from, *mon ami*, it is both.

And your particular field?

Generally, problems of the mind. Specifically, yours.

Jack's cigarette arcs out over the balustrade. But we're getting ahead of ourselves, he says. Feel free to take notes. Let us invent a pair of provost soldiers patrolling the liberated hill villages around Assoro.

Jack begins filling in your blanks. In an abandoned olive grove, he says, the provosts literally trip over you.

You are barely conscious, hiding in the roots of a tree, dehydrated, severely sunburnt. You wear what little remains of your khaki; your tin hat, rifle, ammo packs nowhere to be seen. Your uniform's insignia and flashings are missing, but judging by the ghost shapes left behind, the provosts hazard a guess: you might be a Canadian, might be a private; both facts you evidently didn't want anyone to know. The provosts are certain of one thing: you are a deserter.

Jack pats his pockets for another cigarette. And if there's one thing I've learned about the military, he says, once a provost, always a judge-and-jury.

In August 1943 the German army pulls off one of the most audacious retreats of the Second World War. In under a week, some 60,000 German troops (along with 75,000 Italians) evacuate Sicily across the Strait of Messina.

Allied forces invaded the island on 10 July, British and Canadians to the south and east, Americans to the west. Four days later, German commanders realize they need an exit plan.

For three weeks, from three directions, the Allies move across the island, the scrambling enemy barely ahead of them. To push the little flags across the map is to realize that everyone is heading for the same back door: the narrowing northeast corner of Sicily and the city of Messina.

The Germans get there first. Ferries run non-stop for six days, transporting the pride of the Reich and their hapless Italian partners across the five kilometres of open straits from Messina to the Italian mainland. By 17 August they are gone.

The Allies eventually chase them all the way up the boot.

What follows for you, Jack continues, is sunburn cream, meals-ready-to-eat, interrogation. You clam up: no name, no rank, no serial number. You offer your inquisitors only blank stares, picked-at plates, fitful sleep.

The evidence accumulates. The inability to provide simple biographical details. The amnesia as to where you were found and how you got there. The compliance, moreover the relief, when you were arrested. The lack of proof that you knew what you were doing when you went AWOL. The likelihood that, rather than deliberate shirking, it was the fog of some personal war that set you wandering off.

The army is preoccupied with chasing Germans across the island. So charges not pressed, case more or less closed. The officer leading the investigation scribbles a last marginal note: *If we shot every coward in our ranks, this would be a very small army.*

Smoke? Jack says.

The early Renaissance painter Cennino Cennini, in his hand-book *Il Libro dell'Arte*, describes a pale orange-red colour—cinabrese—as being a mix of sinopia (known as Venetian red) together with a Florentine pigment called bianco San Giovanni (St. John's white). He declares the resulting dusty pink ideal "for painting faces, hands, and nudes on walls . . ."

What Cennini does not mention is that cinabrese is also ideal for tinting a building's exterior stucco. It is a common archi-tectural colour (along with warm whites, pale blues, and a range of yellows, oranges, and reds) throughout the Mediterranean, and has been for millennia.

Jack one-hands his Zippo, lights your cigarette, continues. Where was I? Right, charges not pressed.

You are transported to an infirmary in Siracusa. The army's so-called diet is replaced with local fare, enough pasta to choke a horse. You gain weight, medical staff attempt a gentler interview approach. Gradually you are more forthcoming, though most of it is nonsense. You speak of corn in Egypt. Of skinny-dipping with someone named Alice. Of the Yellow Brick Road.

Soon enough you are transferred here to Taormina and the Villa Rossa. Meanwhile, inquiries continue regarding MIAs or KIAs in the region, personnel otherwise unaccounted for. A tally of names and pertinent records is forwarded.

It isn't red, you say.

The villa?

More warm pink. Cinabrese, if memory serves.

You might mention that to the baroness, Jack says.

Your paperwork landed on my desk, Jack says. Quite the pile. Dates, last known whereabouts, physical descriptions, annotations regarding distinguishing marks, provost reports, interrogation transcripts, an in-tray full of etceteras.

Genesis, you say.

Sorry?

Genesis 42, verse 2: And Jacob said, Behold, I have heard that there is corn in Egypt: get you down thither, and buy for us from thence; that we may live, and not die.

I'm not following.

Means Gran's flop was a wild card.

You and Jack become regulars on the terrace. He brings the coffee, you smoke his cigarettes, the baroness's furniture sags a little further, complains a little louder.

Jack explains that the path of least resistance is for him to simply ask questions. What you remember of the fighting, how you ended up hiding under a tree in the middle of nowhere, what happened to your uniform.

Questions beget questions. What you did before the war, were you close to your parents, what does Gran's love of Shakespeare mean to you, who was Alice.

Is, you say.

Alice?

My *wife*. Imagine the luck.

Weeks on. You accuse Jack of being deliberately obtuse. You tell him of a recent nightmare: you are riding in a car, the brakes have failed, you are heading for a cliff, and Jack—grinning like a carnival clown—is the one behind the wheel.

Jack discourages your use of metaphor, explaining that he is not *that* kind of psychiatrist. Things are what they are, he says, cigars nothing more than cigars. But just out of interest, he says, professional curiosity if you will: What make of car am I driving?

There are mornings when you evade Jack's queries; you equivocate, change the subject, refuse to answer. Afternoons when you ramble from inconsistent to lucid. Jack offers no judgment, his observations considered, unbiased, wise. He assures you that the army need know nothing of your conversations.

And no, Jack says, you cannot read my case notes.

You count the number of conversations with as many morning cappuccinos, as many sundowners, as many packs of Navy Cut. You meet the baroness, a woman rather different than you had pictured: more pantomime chorus than noblesse oblige, all topped with an extraordinary sun hat.

At times you worry these conversations will carry on indefinitely, that one day Jack will give up, proclaim you beyond help or hope. The army will ship you home in a straitjacket.

Until the evening you realize the truth is the only answer left to you.

Jack finishes his *digestivo*, opens his notebook. Think of a clock, he says.

No metaphors, you say.

Humour me.

Jack clears his throat, begins to read.

Subject H, male, mid-twenties, was challenged on his theory of inverting time, his desire to "turn back the clock." Did he actually think it might work? If so, at which point, in what instant, would he stop the hands, set them turning counter?

Was it the moment the provosts lowered their weapons, pushed aside the underbrush, asked him what they should have seen?

Was it the night, the nights, he spent wandering across battle-scarred fields; straining to hear a distant rumbling, the sound of a war moving on, a war managing to forget he had gone missing?

Or was it the day, the days, he spent huddled in summer-dry riverbeds, drinking from fetid puddles? Hiding as the lines of haggard men, women, and children returned to their destroyed villages, their animals balking at the stench of a deserter wafting from a roadside ditch.

Was it subject H's first night in the ravine below the village? Covering himself in deadfall, biting at the threads holding his rank insignia, thinking that if someone found him, they would just move on, dismiss him as a *nessuno*, a nobody.

Was it the moment he escaped the village's maze of alleyways, chest heaving, heels digging in as he fell into the ravine?

The moment he turned a blind corner and realized the snipers were shooting at someone else?

Or the moment he threw away his rifle?

Subject H was asked to pinpoint the moment he started running from the piazza. Did he remember sidestepping a pool of blood? Was it *before* or *after* the bullet embedded itself in the church doors on the other side of the piazza?

Was it the instant when everything went silent, when he closed his eyes, when he pulled the trigger?

Was it *before* or *after* he saw—what? a German? a villager? a blur?—suddenly appear out of the smoke and dust? Was it *before* or *after* he managed to unstick the bolt on his rifle and jam a round into the chamber?

Was it the seconds of panic, the pounding growing louder and faster in his ears, his sweating hands pulling, pushing, forcing the bolt back and forth again and again and again?

Or was it when he heard someone yelling for fuck's sake shoot something?

Subject H was invited to speculate. If reversing time were all it required, how far back would he let it run?

To the moonless night when his squad crawled through an overgrown ravine? Clinging to the near-vertical slope, chirping like insects in the blackness, signalling each other about a goat track leading to the village?

To the army's march from the coast? To everyone being told to space themselves as they crossed the fields, to mark their steps among the mines, to keep their ears open for the threat of ambush, to not touch the booby-trapped wreckage of a retreating enemy? To coughing up the incessant dust? To the silhouette of Mount Etna, heat-hazed and constant in the distance?

Or would it be when the ramp fell open, revealing the thin streak of sunrise along the beach? To the moment he stepped off the landing craft, legs straining to touch bottom? Or to wading ashore, his shoulder bent against a hail of metal that never materialized?

Subject H, you say. Very clinical.

Old habits, Jack says. Let's come at this another way: Suppose you never get on that troopship. Then imagine your sister—Bess, is it?—spending her day, rather than being jostled by crowds of soldiers and well-wishers at the train station, instead sitting for a portrait drawn by her brother.

Suppose your near-sighted, near-tenured deferments come through. Or the closest you get to a recruiting office is passing by, mildly amused by the overuse of exclamation points on the posters.

Imagine an icy Saturday morning.

Alice wraps your scarf around her neck and stamps her feet into a pair of galoshes two sizes too large. She stands at your apartment door, fidgeting, giggling, bouncing like a four-year-old. Well, professor? *Well?*

You raise your hands in mock surrender; set aside the stack of essays to be marked. You ask whose grandmother happened to knit that scarf for whose favourite grandson.

Only grandson, she says.

You gently push Alice out the door ahead of you. She laughs when you ask if she has any intention of being an adult. She turns, kisses you full on.

How's *that* for adult, she says.

You curse her Christmas windows all the way down the stairs.

Alice's arm through yours, you wade through the crowds of holiday shoppers. You hear a commotion off to your right, the sound of car horns, of yelling. You turn your head in time to watch a truck slide through the intersection.

In one graceful motion you slip your arm free, grab Alice's waist, pull her back from the curb.

So, Jack says, run it all backwards.

At which point are you certain? When do you rest, knowing that Alice will live to see her windows? That the army will decline your enlistment. That the Japanese air force will turn its attention elsewhere; the two of you will fight the mice in an East Village bedsit. That in a distant future you might visit Sicily together.

That the girl in the piazza survives.

Perhaps it is the moment you finally believe a village firefight and an icy street and a one-armed husband watching his wife slip away were all turns of fate, accidents, the cruellest of luck, take your pick. Or the moment you realize there was nothing you could have done.

Madrid, 1651. King Philip IV and his wife, Mariana of Austria, welcome their first child, the Infanta Margarita Teresa. Meanwhile the country's pre-eminent artist, Diego Velázquez, has returned to the Spanish court after three years in Italy.

Velázquez completes a number of portraits of the Infanta, painting her likeness at various ages and in various finery. The most enchanting, however, renders her not as spotlit prima donna but as sharing the stage with a bustling chorus.

*Las Meninas* (The ladies-in-waiting), painted in 1656, depicts five-year-old Margarita among a retinue of maids, courtiers, chaperones, bodyguards, dwarfs, the requisite royal dog. Moreover, Velázquez puts himself in the scene, working a large canvas: yet another portrait of Philip and Mariana, goes the theory, their mirrored reflections hovering over their sweet Infanta's shoulder.

Margarita's face—toddler-plump, framed by translucent hair—greets the viewer with a modest hint of a smile. The profile of her tiny torso gently arcs out to silken white panniers and skirts. She is the definition of focal point: a graceful calm in a sycophantic whirlwind.

Discharge paperwork on the terrace. Jump-seat Jeep to Catania, short hops to Malta, Tunis, Algiers; finally to Gibraltar. Below decks to Quebec, third-class to Toronto. The step off the train, your sister's embrace, her daughter in hand. The news about Gran.

In her sleep, Bess says. Six months ago.

Why wasn't I told?

We couldn't find you, she says. And even if we had, damn you, what would you have done? Five thousand miles away, how could you possibly have made me feel less alone?

You kneel, eye-level with Bess's daughter. This must be Maggie, you say. I knew a Maggie once; everyone called her Margarita.

You're forgiven, Bess says. Gran would be happy, knowing you survived.

You lean through the car's window, kiss your niece's perfect blond head.

Gran's flat. You inhale the disinfectant, sneeze out the mustiness, straighten the doilies. Milk and half a loaf of bread in the icebox, courtesy of Bess's ration stamps. Hash-marked dates and measures still climb the kitchen door frame. *The Histories of William Shakespeare* lies open (*Henry IV*, Falstaff's soliloquy) on a side table; a worn pack of cards within easy reach on a bookshelf. She might have just stepped out to run an errand.

In your old bedroom, a few copied canvases, your better efforts. Stretched bed linens against the wall, maps rolled under the bed. Brueghel's peasants, Rembrandt's Lucretia, *Shipwreck at Sea*.

Your Gardner, in need of dusting, sits on the windowsill. You sweep your hand across the curled and yellowing corners protruding from its pages, a farmer measuring the height of his crop.

You look out to the lakefront, try to picture the umbrella pines and the Mediterranean. You exhale, suddenly aware you've been holding your breath, hunching your shoulders against the muffled hum in your head. A year on, no less deafening.

Sunnyside is alive with its July crowds; beach, bathing pavilion, pool all shoulder-to-shoulder. You lift the window. Carousel music, midway hawking, roller-coaster squeals drift up from the amusement park. You wonder if there are fewer couples riding the Lover's Express this season.

The phone rings: Bess on the line, reminding you of Gran's grave number.

She comments on your weight, wondering what the army might be feeding her young prince. She fumbles in the pockets of her apron, curses, finally finds a cigarette. She lights a match, cups her hands to shield the flame, squints as the smoke curls toward her eye.

That's some cough, Gran.

She waves you off, demanding assurance that you are looking in on your sister. Bess has been struggling, she says, since getting the telegram from the war department. A widow at her age, it breaks the heart. She'll be needing help with Maggie. Mind you provide it.

She asks after Alice. Not your fault, she says.

As Gran reminds you to water the plants and take out the trash, you place a bouquet of day lilies on her marker.

The fall term begins, you return to work. In the faculty lounge, a round or two of hail-the-conquering-hero. Pats on the back land heavy. Too many toasts, too many innocent questions, too many mentions of your greying temples.

You decline to provide details of what they call your overseas adventures. Loose lips and all that, you say. You do mention the relentless heat and dust.

In the quad, postgrads (you could swear they were juniors when you left) call out versions of welcome home professor as they breeze past. The best you can manage is awkward smiles and half-waves.

The crunch in your neck, the stoop in your spine, the clicks in your knees: reminders of an overgrown ravine, of dry river-beds, of the hardscrabble of dead olive groves. Of you closing in on thirty, already ancient.

The Age of Reason moves European thinking from super-stition and unquestioned religious doctrine toward scien-tific discipline and irrefutable fact. From Descartes's "I think therefore I am" to the French Revolution, logic gradually supersedes emotion.

It is not necessarily so. Francisco Goya's etching *The Sleep of Reason Produces Monsters* (*c.* 1799) depicts a man (an artist?) slumped over a desk covered with pens and paper (drawing materials?). Hovering around him are his so-called night monsters—bats, owls, cats—suggesting that a creative mind, no matter how logical, cannot escape its horrors.

At the age of twenty-four, Gustave Courbet paints his own portrait. Known as *The Desperate Man* (*c.* 1843), it shows the French realist in the desperate grip of madness. Terrified eyes bulge unseeing, gnarled hands tear at his hair. In time, a more mature Courbet will commit to changing the art world, to rejecting his Romantic forebears, to putting the unvarnished truth of life on canvas. But here, at the beginning of his career, Courbet confesses a personal truth: here is the artist battling the all-too-emotional demons of insecurity.

The Shoreview, a Sunday afternoon, a knock at the door.

Since returning, you have made headway transforming Gran's flat. Retired to closets are the armrest doilies, the floral wall-papers, the needlepointed Blue Boy; a good woman's touch given over to claustrophobic junk shop. The plants have been dead for a while.

In assorted stages of completion: forged Titians shoved in corners, replica Géricaults hung cockeyed here and there, dotted Seurats propped on the radiators. Spent tubes of paint gather in corners, tinned fans of brushes hold the doors open, splattered drop cloths and newspapers cover furniture and floor.

You open the door. Bess stands on the landing, pie in hand. She cautiously steps past you, the smell of apples and cinnamon wafting in her wake.

Where's Maggie? you say.

With her grandparents, Bess says. Could we possibly open a window?

What *is* that smell?

Bess waves away the kitchen air. Still affecting the tortured genius, she says. Ladies and gentlemen, my brother the walking cliché. Let us admire his various skills and expertise.

—culinary acumen limited, tinned goods a staple (provided opener is readily at hand). Eggs scrambled or not at all.

—collects a sinkful of dishes in less than a week; takes up washing only as cups cabinet runs bare

—wouldn't know business end of mop if life depended on it

—can light stove if given enough notice to locate matches

—preferred appliance: kettle. Adept at reusing tea leaves.

According to medieval medicine, an excess of black bile (one of the body's four humours) results in melancholia. The patient experiences inexplicable pains, hallucinations, a so-called "darkened" mind.

In 1514 Albrecht Dürer produces *Melencolia I*, a monochrome portrait of the condition as winged woman. She is despondent, her head in her hands. Scattered around her are the tools of a Renaissance mind. Yet these tools are idle. Some have theorized the woman's misery is the price she pays for her unbalanced humours, for a lack of inspiration, for her fear that the ideas will not come. Others believe the engraving represents one of Dürer's own tenets: to be an artist is to be more than a little mad.

In 1738 Samuel Johnson writes to a friend: "when I rise my breakfast is solitary, the black dog waits to share it, from breakfast to dinner he continues barking. . . ." Where Johnson first encounters the term *black dog* is unknown, but it is likely he is aware of its mythic connections (guardians of the underworld, jackal-headed death deities, etc.). Johnson is also well aware of Robert Burton's *Anatomy of Melancholy* (published in 1621). He may have used Burton's 900-page tome as bedtime reading, hoping to cure his insomnia—ironically brought on by his melancholy.

May 1945. Classes cancelled.

You weave your way through the student crowds waving their GERMANY SURRENDERS headlines and Union Jacks. All is sunshine, trees budding, reserve giving way to release. There's dancing in the quad, kissing strangers, impromptu songs: "I'm Waiting, Soldier Boy." There may even be a bounce in your step. After all, you have kept calm, carried on, survived.

Yet the more you reassure yourself, the blacker the dog.

It arrives without warning: anytime, anywhere, callous, cruel. Only the tells are dependable—cold sweat in the small of your back, stomach butterflies turning to cramps, breathing shallowing to a wheeze. Soon enough the vise grips your chest, the hammer splits your forehead; the desperation that there is nowhere to hide, that someone will notice.

The visions, the terrors: colourless. Beginning as dull sepia, only to drain to blacks and whites. There are no lively pastels to divert your attention; no comforting hues. All is blinding glare and unnerving shadow.

From the French *gris* (grey), grisaille describes the technique of painting using only a palette of blacks and whites and their gradients. Throughout history, artists have used the approach for underpaintings (creating a base for subsequent layers of colour), to imitate the three-dimensional appearance of sculpture (particularly bas-relief), or as a preliminary guide for an engraver's reproduction.

The technique is considered a test of artistic skill, mimicking the monochrome drawings of Renaissance masters. By removing extraneous detail and the distraction of colour, the artist has no crutch to lean on, nowhere to hide.

With grisaille, details sharpen, contrasts heighten, the subject appears in its essence. Yet the finished work can appear cold. Thus some artists have been known to underscore their monochromes with warmer tones: the result being like the faded truths of old sepia photographs or yellowing newspapers.

A spring term lecture: monochromatics. You finalize your notes.

*1: grisaille definition, 2: history. Q's: Absence of colour—to what end? Blacks, whites, greys—details refined or muddy, effects raw or sepia?*

In class, your opening will concern the Zen paintings of seventeenth-century Japan,

*touch on measured elegance, meditative simplicity leading to enlightenment. Mention flawless blacks, calligraphic brushwork*

You will move on to Ingres,

*discuss how Ing. restricts his own palette, ties his own hands, challenges himself to take a greyscale run at his Grand Odalisque*

Then to Whistler,

*reference JMW's constraint, his elimination of the unnecessary. Tonal/spatial harmony. Examples: The Andalusian, Artist's Mother?*

1937 and Spain is in the second year of civil war. Nazi-backed Nationalists battle an alliance of Republican factions, including Basque loyalists. April 26: the town of Guernica (spiritual capital of Basque country, considered a bastion of Republican resistance) is attacked by a combined German/Italian air force.

It is market day, Monday, late afternoon. As most of Guernica's male population are away at war, it is primarily women and children who gather in the town centre.

Without warning or provocation, repeated bombing runs (using conventional and incendiary explosives) reduce the town to an inferno. Attempts to escape the firestorm are thwarted by the shattered bridges and cratered roads leading out of town. Anyone seeking refuge in surrounding fields is gunned down by strafing fighter planes.

It is not known how many civilian lives are lost. The Nationalists put the number at barely one hundred, the Republicans inflate the toll into the thousands. Either way, the bombing prompts international condemnation: the French newspapers *Ce Soir* and *L'Humanité* each run front-page stories, blaming Hitler and Mussolini for the slaughter.

You will close with *Guernica*.

The mural has been travelling since its unveiling at the 1937 World's Fair: London, San Francisco, New York. You have seen the magazine articles, read the reviews, studied the photographs. At first look the mural is a manic exercise of cubist editorializing. Closer inspection reveals a monochromatic reportage, including the use of hash marks simulating a yellowing newspaper. Picasso as journalist, says a critic.

The work is some eleven feet high, twenty-six feet wide. To fit it in Gran's flat, let alone copy it, you would need to knock out a wall, probably add a mezzanine. Even then, there would be the matter of the size of delivery van required to move the mural to your lecture hall. You rethink: work it up in sections, the most compelling details. You stretch two canvases.

Your eye turns first to Picasso's dying horse, illuminated by a childlike rendering of a bare light bulb. You focus on the animal's screaming muzzle, the knifelike tongue, the flared nostrils. You feel uneasy, but you cannot look away.

The attack comes on as you work up your second canvas, the *Pietà* at the extreme left of the mural. A wailing woman, her head thrown back in grief, cradles her child's lifeless body.

Your brush begins to shake, at first an imperceptible twitch. You grip your wrist, steady your hand. Then a pounding between your ears, a flickering vision.

You are in the village piazza, hovering above the scene. Below you: slow-motion soldiers run in circles and trace the pattern of the cobblestones. You are floating in a whirlwind of smoke and dust. Beneath your feet: the body of a small girl, lying on her back and staring up at you.

Your head falls back, mouth agape. You hear yourself shouting for a medic while a pool of blood blossoms around the girl. Everything is colourless: the blood oily and black.

In the first decade of the twentieth century, the Fauvist movement captures the art world's attention. Characterized by aggressive composition and palettes, influenced by African tribal aesthetics, the movement is named for a group of avant-garde artists—the so-called Wild Beasts—including Henri Matisse.

His *Portrait of Madame Matisse* (a.k.a. *The Green Stripe*), painted in 1905, comes to represent the best (for some, the worst) Fauvism has to offer. A portrait of his wife, Amélie, the work is nicknamed for the olive-green band vertically dividing the woman's face, hairline to chin.

The portrait is a hallmark of Fauvism: saturated, otherworldly, jarring. Matisse's juxtaposition of colour opposites—reds against greens, purples bordering oranges—only magnifies the painting's energy. It is thought the artist's intention was to mimic three dimensions without using the conventional techniques of highlight and shade.

For all its innovation, critics call *The Green Stripe* disturbing, demented, strange, and terrible. Some theories go so far as to suggest the Matisses may have been having marital troubles at the time, driving Henri to take his frustrations out on Amélie.

December 1962. Alice gone twenty years. A freezing drizzle glazes the city. No telling how thick the crowds will be downtown, how many wives will be distracted by the holiday windows, how many husbands will open their door to find a nervous constable dripping on the mat.

You are sitting to the window side of a lecture theatre. Today's topic: "Matisse, the Fauvist Years," a symposium of university nabobs, doctoral candidates, theorists, gallerists. The day wears on, the weather deteriorates, ice pellets tick against the windows.

You glance out the window. Alice is laughing, wrestling that heavy, itchy scarf; slipping in the wet, trying to keep her balance.

In the hall outside the theatre, gripping your knees to keep them from giving way, you assure the organizer that of course you'll be giving tomorrow's keynote, it must have been something you ate, there's no need to fuss.

Crossing the quad, you notice a figure walking a few strides ahead, coattails flapping in the winter gusts. You try to place the familiarity: the determined gait, the slump-shouldered silhouette, the spectacles balanced on a balding head. The figure pauses for a moment, pats his pockets, removes a glove, one-hands a Zippo. He turns around.

Thought that might be you, Jack says, picking tobacco off his lip.

I could use one of those, you say.

Have this one. Been trying to quit since the war. Success is proving elusive.

Time enough for a coffee?

Anything to get out of this weather.

The Goethe Prize rewards significant achievement in the literary arts. Most recipients are writers first and foremost, but from time to time the prize recognizes individuals from other fields. In 1930, Dr. Sigmund Freud receives the accolade, not for medicine, but for literature.

While pioneering therapeutic approaches in mental health, including the then radical use of psychoanalysis, Freud is also a gifted storyteller. The literary techniques in his essays, opinions, and case notes—multiple points of view, flashbacks, digressions, non-sequential plotting—lead critics to declare his writing to be as much novelistic as analytic, refreshingly more Proustian than pathological.

In 1932 the prize committee again honours Freud, this time for career-spanning contributions to psychology and German literary culture. A year later, at the urging of Joseph Goebbels, Freud's books are burned by the German Student Union.

Two stools at the counter, what'll it be gents, cuppa joe coming up. You ask Jack what brings him to Toronto.

Quick in-and-out, he says. Guest lecture for the pimply undergrads: "Writing a Better Case Study." Back to Montreal on the evening train.

Still shrinking heads?

Keeping a hand in. You? Judging by the need for a razor and the anemic pallor, you appear to be sleeping as poorly as you did in Taormina.

That was a long time ago.

Luckily my train's not till six.

An hour in and Jack hasn't interrupted, annotated, footnoted, asked a question. Then,

I hear the baroness has renovated.

Sorry?

This Gardner of yours. The idea has merit. Put one's demons in context, explain the inexplicable, rationalize the nonsense. Here's another idea: Ever thought about going back?

Absolutely not.

Think again, my friend. Confront the black dog in situ. Tighten the leash, bring it to heel. Retrace your steps, fill the gaps in your memory, close the gestalt circle. In army parlance, declare a truce with your ghostly hound.

That's a lot of metaphors.

Thanks. I've been practising.

Look at it this way, Jack says. Try taking some credit for surviving.

There's plenty who made it home in one piece.

And how many had their wives die on them? How many had that bottomless pit open in front of them and chose not to take the easy way out? How many pulled themselves together, kept going, did their bit? How many remembered the best of the times they had with those women, rather than dreading the times without them?

Marble is formed by geological forces of pressure and heat altering the structure of sedimentary or igneous rock. The result is a soft, sculptural material, easily worked when freshly quarried, ideal for fine detail and high polish, with a low density that allows light to penetrate the stone. In expert hands, marble can appear as alive as human skin, as gossamer as a veil.

Bernini's *Ecstasy of Saint Teresa* is considered a masterpiece of such illusion. Yet no sculpture accomplishes the *trompe l'oeil* better than *The Veiled Virgin*, carved in the 1850s by the Milanese sculptor Giovanni Strazza.

It is a bust of the young Virgin Mary: frozen in prayer, eyes closed, chin demurely tucked. Her features, despite being cloaked in fabric, are a mirage of grace. One can literally see through her marble veil.

Summer, 1963. Rome invaded by hordes of holy men electing a Pope, art historians giving up their off-terms by conferencing new ways to teach their charges back home. The Eternal City in July: everyone battles the heat, huddles in shady colonnades, wades in fountains. Locals have decamped to the beaches or the Apennines or hunkered down in front of a fan.

Brownies at the ready, red-robed cardinals pose in front of the Castel Sant'Angelo. Per diem'd academics dribble gelato down the front of their summer-weights on the Spanish Steps. You prefer the ghetto near Campo de' Fiori: fewer touts, fewer tourists; meals reasonable and generous; plenty of history in the cool of narrow alleyways.

Yours is the closing presentation of the week's conference: "The Art of Deception: Marble Drapery from Bernini to Strazza." Chilly reception from the Italians, polite applause from the Brits, when's the bar open from the Americans.

Late afternoon and the haze of faculty wine weighs heavy as you run to catch a tram. The relentless sun, the reeking gutters, the pavement heaving underfoot. The last time you were in Rome, a postgrad pilgrim in a mouldy *pensione*, the weather never seemed this oppressive.

The street begins to shift: better you sit down before you fall down. You stumble across the tram tracks to a small café opposite, clutch at an empty chair. Under their awning, the waiters have been watching. One approaches with a carafe. *Acqua, signore?*

You drain the bottle. It returns in monochrome fits and starts: the olive grove, the dappled sun through the branches, the provost holding out a canteen.

Ever thought of going back, *signore*?

You're confused by the quizzical look on the waiter's face. Why his suddenly perfect English? A young couple on a passing Vespa return your glass-eyed stare as they ride past.

Across the street a line of tradesmen and housemaids waits for the tram, regards you like an operatic chorus. Their pleading hands reach for you, their voices beseeching an invisible audience to pass judgment, to show mercy. The years, they sing; the sleeplessness, the black memories, the need for absolution, for forgiveness. Is this man's suffering not worthy of redemption?

The tram pulls away; the chorus disappears. The Vespa couple drive on, happy and oblivious. In English, you ask the waiter for directions to the nearest telegraph office. He shakes his head. *Non capisco, signore.*

*Per favore,* you say. *Taormina?*

The winner of the 1907 Paris-to-Peking automobile race is an Italian aristocrat, Prince Scipione Borghese. His car, an Itala manufactured in Turin, is painted a fresh-blood red.

The same year, Grand Prix organizers codify national motor-racing colours: blue for France, yellow for Belgium, green for Great Britain, red for the United States (until a red Fiat wins the 1907 French Grand Prix and Italy claims the colour). Eventually Germany abandons its lead-based white, as it adds too much weight to its vehicles.

Between the wars it seems every Italian automobile, Alfa to Fiat to Maserati, can be purchased in Borghese's *rosso corsa* (racing red). Enzo Ferrari adopts the colour as the signature livery for all his cars, though in later years there will be any number of shades of "Ferrari red."

Rome to Catania: the pilot treats passengers to a once-around flyby of Etna. A bouncy landing and you wait for an hour on the tarmac while the ground crew positions the stairs, then repositions, then repositions again. From the airport to Taormina, a local bus, full to bursting, you in the aisle the whole way, shifting from foot to foot in lieu of a toilet.

The brochures tell the truth: Villa Rossa has been renovated to good effect. Terrace slates levelled, balustrade sandblasted, the sun-baked cinabrese refreshed. New loungers, attentive staff, and, judging by the tennis whites and crisp linens parading through the lobby, a clientele that left their Capri reservations until too late.

The coffee has not changed, nor, it appears, has the baroness. Some things are timeless, she says, kissing you on both cheeks.

The next morning, the concierge hands you the keys to your rental car. He wishes you a safe journey, explains that it has been an extraordinarily dry summer, the roads should be passable, no more than a couple of hours and you should arrive at your destination.

The rental is a vibrant red, *certo*.

Amid the complaining gears and an indecisive clutch, you white-knuckle the wheel, expecting the next switchback to bring on your visions: tiptoeing through another minefield, sleeping in a dead riverbed, crawling on hand and knee toward a stronghold rising in a starless sky.

Some things are timeless.

But if nothing changes on this island, why is nothing familiar? You tap the brakes, coast past sunburnt flatland you might have crossed twenty years ago. You downshift, engine straining to reach another village you might have searched alley by alley, doorway by doorway, hunting for an enemy on the run.

Three hours in. On a rare straight and level stretch of road you see an old man in the distance. You slow to pass him by then pull over. The rental, caked in dust, backfires to a stop.

You spread a map across the ticking hood, light a cigarette. The old man comes up beside you. The two of you stare at the map like some lost vaudevillian duo, the old fellow wearing the Stan Laurel grin, reaching under his cap to scratch his head.

You ask directions. Your tuneless Italian prompts no response. You try the language of tobacco. *Canadese*, he says with a toothless smile, flipping the smoke to his mouth. Then the banter of mimed gestures, smiles and frowns, nods of the head.

You point at the map, name the village. He slides your finger to the north and west of Assoro. *Vicino*, he says. Near.

You hand him your pack of cigarettes. *Cent'anni*, he says over his shoulder, tipping his cap and walking back the way he came.

It takes a moment. *Cent'anni*, a hundred years of health.

A rise in the road and there it is, lifting out of the flats. Twenty years ago you saw that distant silhouette as the sun was setting, the light fading, the sky moving toward a moonless, ominous night.

The hill's obtuse triangle: the gentle western slope, the steep eastern rampart. The village impossibly perched on top, campanile peaking above the warren of buildings crowding the summit. A village no different from a thousand others, but the one you remember as though it were yesterday.

It is said that the heart of an Italian community is its campanile. Ornate and circular, sober and square, these bell towers are both utilitarian (summoning the faithful) and architectural anchors; historical, cultural, communal touchstones.

Pisa has one that famously leans; arguably the most iconic stands in the Piazza San Marco in Venice. Siena's campanile boasts six bells and is striped in courses of black and white stone to match its cathedral. There is a campanile in Messina complete with an enormous astronomical clock, wherein a system of weights and gears drives a whirligig performance featuring merry-go-round figures, biblical scenes, a bronze lion, and a rooster that flaps its wings then crows as the clock strikes twelve.

The largest city can have dozens. The poorest hilltop hamlet can have one: windowless, faced in rough stone, in need of repointing, squaring up. Humble in its reach for heaven and wanting a good wash.

Someday, a colleague in the faculty lounge will ask what you hoped to find by going back. You will have no answer, nor will you be able to explain how it felt walking through that village two decades on. You will only say that, whatever it was, it was nothing like what you found.

You step into the piazza. The space feels larger than you remember, more sloped, more crooked polygon than perfect square, one end anchored by the steps of the village church and its campanile. The piazza's ancient cobbles, radiating from a small fountain, still firm underfoot. Spokes to the fountain's wheel, stone benches stay cool in the shade of young pistachio trees.

Silence, stillness; the air does not move. Old companions return: the claustrophobia, the panic of being trapped, not knowing where to run, of hunching your shoulders against a hail of metal.

Your mind's eye becomes a bird's eye at the top of the campanile, looking down at you, crouching in the midst of a cyclone: gunfire, mortar blasts, concussion grenades, FORFUCK'SSAKE SHOOTSOMETHING. Clouds of exploding plaster, shards of broken masonry caught in the whirlwind. The church façade pocked with bullet holes, windows shattering. Raked lines of machine gun fire lift the cobbles.

A girl appears through the smoke. She is chasing a blur, holding her hands over her ears. Her mouth is open, there is no voice.

She came out of nowhere, Alice.

You watch yourself sidestep a pool of black as you run past the girl's body.

*Buongiorno, signore.*

You turn to see a woman closing the church doors behind her. Dark eyes, features weathered by wind and sun, a mane of dark hair streaked with grey.

You have seen that face, that hair somewhere before. A younger version, perhaps. Your mind flips through images, finds it in Leonardo's notebooks. His unfinished study, *La Scapigliata*, the Lady with Dishevelled Hair.

She asks where you are from, smiles at your accented Italian. Welcome back, she says.

You hear the sound of giggling behind the church doors. The woman's smile disappears. *Silenzio*, she calls out.

She offers her hand. Pazienza.

Henry. Sorry, have we met?

A few of your countrymen visit from time to time. Boys then, fighting their grown-up war. Men now, dragging their wives on battlefield tours, telling tall tales. We assumed you were one of them. Did you liberate our village?

Others did the liberating. We?

The orphans. I am their teacher. Can we be of assistance?

Was there always a fountain here?

It was built after the war. A memorial.

To?

Follow me.

Nuremberg, the sixteenth century. Sebald Beham is a leading force in the Little Masters, a group of young artists following the creative footsteps of Albrecht Dürer. Behan produces almost two thousand engravings, etchings, and woodcuts; most are postage-stamp small and highly detailed. He works with a range of subjects, including biblical portraits, scenes of peasant life, and classical myths.

Including that of *Patientia* (1540). Behan's engraving depicts her as winged allegory: the ultimate guardian of the innocent. She sits on a fluted column, toga'd in the manner of Athens or Rome. Her legs calmly crossed at the knee, she cuddles a sleeping lamb (itself a traditional symbol) in her lap. Lurking behind, a fanged, wart-covered demon attempts, to no avail, to spirit the animal away.

Pazienza leads you through the village. You ask about her name.

It means patience, she says. A virtue my father claimed I should have inherited from my mother. He took care of the cemetery. After she died, I became his assistant.

You compliment her English.

My father couldn't read or write, she says, but he knew enough to send his daughter away to university. Rome, before the war. When I returned, the church needed help with the orphans. I've been caring for them ever since. And you?

Also a teacher. Not much of a soldier, though.

No tall tales? No wife tagging along? Then why come back?

I'm not sure, you say.

You reach a spur of hilltop at the edge of the village. A high masonry wall, stretching along the height, blocks any view. Set in the wall, a pair of ornate iron gates. Pazienza wipes the orange rust on her apron as she pushes them open.

Perhaps the reason you came is in here, she says.

The village's cemetery fans out from the gates. Groomed paths named for the apostles, bordered with hedge work, run between sections meticulously halved, quartered, eighth'd. Everywhere are mausoleums like Lilliputian villas, marital crypts with inset portraits, ornate headstones, simple markers. Vaults are solid and squared, markers are perfectly levelled, not a weed in sight. It is a miniature city clinging to the hilltop, its skyline painted in shades of creams, chalks, pale greys, blacks.

You look out over the cemetery to the valley below. Far to the east, clouds veil the upper reaches of Etna, threatening rain.

Pazienza leads you to a section of rough-hewn markers. Set flush to the ground, the stones carry eroded inscriptions: the shadows of names, dates, epitaphs. Unreadable, as good as blank.

She tells you that before the Germans arrived, her father would use the finest marble and granite quarried from across the island. Then came the war. Finding proper stones became impossible. She would help her father scrounge the ravines below the village. What they found needed to be light enough to carry, but were often too soft to hold a chisel mark or withstand the weathering.

The stones you cannot read, she says, mark the graves of those who died during the war. My father kept no records, instead memorizing who was buried where. I became his bookkeeper.

It was the least we could do. We had been village talismans long before the war, beads in our neighbours' rosaries.

It was not enough that my father dug our neighbours' graves or that I tended their crypts: we were their guarantee. If we bore witness to their burials, they might slip past Saint Peter unchallenged. No matter how heavy their debts, how grievous their sins, how few their friends. No matter what kind of life they had lived.

When I was away in Rome, the village worried itself to distraction. Not that I might come to harm or fall from grace, but that they might die while I was away.

My father and I renewed the ritual after I came home, attending to burials whether we knew the deceased or not. We kept our distance, echoed the priest's final amen, waited until all the mourners had left before sealing a tomb or filling a hole.

Charon's obol (from *obolos*, a denomination of ancient Greek currency) describes the money placed on, sometimes in, the mouth of a dead person before burial. Mythology defines the coin as payment to the Greek god Charon, the underworld ferryman who guided the souls of the dead across the River Styx.

The phrase *Charon's obol* can also serve as archaeological shorthand for the variety of items buried with the deceased or placed on their grave marker. Coins, stones, personal possessions, mementoes, poems, love notes, etc.; in theory these would ease the passage to the afterlife.

Charon's obol is sometimes referred to in Latin as *viaticum*, meaning "sustenance for the journey"; a coin on the mouth both protecting the soul of the dead on its travels and preventing its haunted return.

There are remembrances scattered throughout the cemetery. Wilted bouquets in need of refreshing, tarnished votive vases. Icons of faded Virgins, mottled photographs of loved ones behind cracked glass, small pebbles, neat rows of coins.

A black stone marker, plain, unpolished, in a corner far from the cemetery gates, catches your eye. There are no offerings, no engravings.

The German, Pazienza says. My father believed everyone deserved a place. No matter the life lived.

The German? you ask.

It was sunset, Pazienza says. My father and I were standing by the gates, watching the burial party. I remember the glow of their cigarettes. Like fireflies.

They were huddled together, their black boots turning white as they shuffled in the dust. They had removed their shirts: their braces hung loose; their undershirts soaked through. Unshaven, uncombed, more bored teenagers than battle-weary fighters. I could smell them from where I stood. Nervous sweat mixing with rotting flesh and burning tobacco.

Their commanding officer stood at the head of the grave, covering his nose and mouth with a handkerchief. In the grave, wrapped in an oily tarp, lay one of his own.

Four days earlier, the commanding officer's driver had gone missing.

Everyone in the village had a theory: the man had stolen a bottle of wine, the mayor's grappa, a flask of schnapps. He had found a sunny corner, a shady garden, a quiet doorway; emptied the bottle and passed out. His resulting sunburn, headache, bladder woke him near midnight. He went looking for a cellar, alleyway, church pew to sleep things off.

A search party was mustered.

Two days passed. The search party gave up and herded the entire village into the piazza. The commanding officer stood on the church steps. I remember him looking broken, as though he suddenly realized what we had known since the day he arrived: even if he could speak our language or dye his blond hair or take up farming or marry the mayor's daughter, he and his men would never be welcome here.

In a jumble of Sicilian and Italian and German, the officer announced that if his driver was not found by evening, we would all be reined to his car. We could then pull him back to Berlin and out of our lives.

In the end it was discovered that the driver had stumbled around in the dark and fallen into a ravine. Judging by the angle of his head when he was found, his neck had snapped as he pinwheeled to the bottom. A bottle was never discovered, but his bladder took the blame anyway: the man's trousers were around his ankles.

A dog found what was left of him, nibbled by the wild pigs that forage the slopes below the village. The ravine was too steep to carry the body out, the search party unnerved by the thought of the pigs. They lashed the body to a donkey; you could hear its harness bell tolling the procession across the whole village. My father and I were waiting at the cemetery.

There were no vacancies among the crypts; burying the man anywhere near the children's ground was unthinkable. My father approached the commanding officer and pointed to a distant corner of the cemetery.

Everyone deserves a place, he said.

Homer describes a sunrise in the *Odyssey* as "rosy-fingered dawn."

Raphael's painting *The Madonna of the Pinks* depicts the infant Jesus presenting a pink flower to the Virgin Mary, symbolizing the spiritual marriage between mother and child.

In the mid-eighteenth century, pastel hues are the height of fashion at the court of Versailles. No hue is more desirable than a dusty pink, doubtless because it is championed by the king's mistress, Madame de Pompadour.

A century later in England, pink is for boys, blue is for girls. Red, according to the Victorians, represents strength, honour, bravery—soldiers wear red, gentlemen likewise. Ergo, boys should wear a youthful version of such a manly colour. (Victorian children of both sexes actually wore mostly white. Coloured fabrics of any hue quickly faded when scrubbed in boiling water.)

The Latin *roseus* describes both the colour and the flower. It is an etymological base for the name Rosa.

A lemon tree shades concentric rows of small markers in the centre of the cemetery. Among the offerings are toys: metal trucks, homemade dolls, carved wooden animals.

No one knows how old this tree is, Pazienza says. One hundred, two hundred years? Do such trees live so long? All anyone knows is that it still bears lemons bigger than your fist, and has cooled the children's ground longer than anyone can remember.

She stops at a marker, smooth as river rock, the engraving long worn away.

She had adopted the church cat, Pazienza says. Reared it from a kitten. The orphans and I were hiding in the cellar, but in the chaos of the fighting, the cat panicked and ran out. Rosa chased after it, into the piazza.

She was eleven.

How long should you stand in front of a child's grave? Is a minute enough? An hour? Do you drop like a pilgrim, wear your knees raw in penitence, pray to a feckless god that thinks nothing of killing the innocent?

Is it wrong to admire the view? The sun lowering across the valley and stretching the shadows below the village? The mass of Etna, silhouetted, barely visible in the distance? The cool shade of an old lemon tree? Do you wish that the child could see, that Alice could see, what you see?

Do you damn the cruelty, the unfairness, the waste? Do you accept the explanation—think of it as collateral damage, the cost of doing business—knowing instead it was murder plain and simple; that an apology, no matter the contrition, excuses nothing, absolves nothing? No matter the life you have lived? How do you confess, tell her it was you who closed his eyes, fired blind? How do you beg forgiveness?

You struggle to breathe. Sobs rack your shoulders, tears streak your face. There are some people you should meet, Pazienza says.

A dozen pairs of eyes widen as Pazienza explains that Signor Henry has come from a place where people live in houses made of snow. A dozen arms fly into the air, straining to be called upon, eager to introduce you to their church cat, sleeping through the commotion on a windowsill.

You make the rounds of the schoolroom, shaking sweaty little hands, admiring cursive exercises, addressing urgent concerns. Pazienza translates: yes, you like their village very much; no, you do not own a cat; yes, you have seen the ocean.

Off by himself, a boy hunches over his desk, oblivious in concentration. Around him are scattered crayons and crumpled balls of paper. You look over his shoulder: a drawing of a ship. Billowed sails, too many masts, dashed lines for cannon fire. *Cristoforo Colombo?* you ask. *Sì*, the boy says.

You survey the desk, find the worn nub of a red crayon. You hand it to the boy and point to the ship's cruciform sail. He eagerly agrees, careful to keep within the lines.

Born in Grenoble in 1836, Henri Fantin-Latour graduates with distinction from the École des beaux-arts in Paris. He hones his talent copying masterpieces in the Louvre. He moves in proper circles, marries well, counts Whistler among his friends. His contemporaries include Manet and Zola. Proust drops his name in *The Guermantes Way*.

For all his fame, Fantin's reputation among art critics hinges on his group portraits of the intellectual elite of the day. But the pundits are not impressed. With rare exception, they dismiss his portraiture as cold; at best sombre, at worst comatose. Even the portrait of his own wife and in-laws lacks emotion, much less love: everyone looks as if they are waiting to see the dentist.

Luckily, Fantin is more than a portraitist. He also paints flowers, in all their arranged abundance. He paints them so well that they make his fortune. In spite of his nationality, he is more famous in London than on *le boulevard*.

Peonies, poppies, chrysanthemums, roses. Intense, near-photographic realism, as though the florist had just delivered. A Fantin flower bursts off the canvas. It may be still, but it is very much alive.

You ask if the boy might lend you some paper. Pazienza leans down and whispers in the boy's ear. A pause, a nod. You choose a pink crayon.

Broad strokes, sure hand, careful shading. An impression, a memory of a lecture, a Fantin rose.

You fold the paper into a square. As neat as origami, as small as the palm of your hand.

Binney & Smith, maker of professional pigments, introduces a line of drawing crayons for the general consumer in 1902. Alice Binney, wife of the company's co-founder, invents the name Crayola for the line, combining the French for chalk (*craie*) with *ola* (as in *oleaginous*: the wax used in making crayons).

The Crayola 64 assortment, introduced in 1958, becomes among Binney & Smith's top sellers. Its iconic yellow-and-green flip-top box, complete with built-in sharpener, contains sixty-four colours arranged in "stadiums"—each row of sixteen slightly higher than the one in front.

While the 64's spectrum changes periodically—hues added or retired, others renamed—two shades of pink stand the tests of time and taste: magenta and carnation pink, known for a time as rose pink.

Consider the years that follow, the disjointed conversations of correspondence, Pazienza's missives archived between the pages of your Gardner, the airmail stamps steamed off and saved for your niece.

You ask after the children; suggest a few artists for their curriculum. Tell them about Van Gogh's ear, you write. They should love it, just creepy enough. You ask if the boxes of crayons arrived.

Pazienza manages a holiday to Taormina. She sends an antique postcard: the view from the Greek theatre was everything you had promised, but the Villa Rossa was much too expensive on a teacher's wages. She did manage a coffee on the terrace.

You write that you'll be attending a conference on Leonardo's notebooks the following summer in Florence. Could we meet?

She responds that the dry sciroccos out of the Sahara are late this year. There has been more rain; the children check the fountain each day. Rosa's drawing is safely where you left it, dry between the stones.

The journals of Marcus Aurelius ultimately run to twelve volumes and include notes and philosophical mementoes intended solely for personal guidance and self-improvement. The entries often take the form of quotations, at times written in the second person, and vary in length from one sentence to several paragraphs. The original journal was never meant for publication and thus has no title. History will call it *Meditations*.

Leonardo da Vinci describes his notebooks as being "without order, drawn from many papers, which I have copied here hoping to arrange them later, each in its place, according to the subjects of which they treat."

Florence? Alice says.

You slip the Taormina postcard somewhere between the Renaissance and the Baroque.

## NOTES.

To list every source the author consulted in the writing of this novel would require more pages than the novel itself, turning what is humble fiction into a bibliographic exercise of mind-numbing proportion. Suffice to say the citations would number in the hundreds. The author is also aware that there is more than one way to write the truth. Thus he has taken liberties: errors in reworking, reimagining, or reinterpreting facts are his alone.

Nonetheless, the following deserve specific mention:

Young Henry recites "Tom Thumb's Alphabet," from *Mother Goose's Nursery Rhymes* (George Routledge and Sons, London, 1877).

Vincent van Gogh's letter to his brother regarding the painting of olive trees is included in *Vincent van Gogh: A Self-Portrait in Art and Letters.*

Captain Parker's diary can be found through the website of the Juno Beach Centre, Normandy, France: www.junobeach.org/ canada-in-wwii/articles/the-invasion-of-sicily/.

*And No Birds Sang*, Farley Mowat's memoir of serving in the Italian campaign, in particular his experiences in Sicily, proved invaluable. As did Mark Zuehlke's military history *Operation Husky: The Canadian Invasion of Sicily*.

The author also owes a literary debt to Simon Schama's *Power of Art*; Julian Barnes's *Keeping an Eye Open: Essays on Art*; Kassia St. Clair's *The Secret Lives of Colour*; and Colum McCann's novel *Apeirogon*.

WITH THANKS.

For early readings, appropriately nitpickish: Erum Shazia Hasan, Nicola Inwood, David Kent, Kim Paglialunga.

For patient representation when others would have abandoned hope years ago: Suzanne Brandreth.

For editorial acumen nonpareil: Martha Kanya-Forstner, Rick Meier.

For the expert crafting of books, particularly this one: Susan Burns, John Sweet, Kelly Hill, Daniella Zanchetta, Gillian Watts, Christie Hanson.

For first readings, general whip-cracking, title approval, and Pazienza: Rebecca Richardson.

And in memoriam: Wayson Choy, Graeme Gibson. Mentors, beacons, gentlemen.

CS RICHARDSON'S first novel, *The End of the Alphabet*, was an international bestseller, published in fourteen countries and ten languages, and won the Commonwealth Writers' Prize for Best First Book (Canada and the Caribbean). His second novel, *The Emperor of Paris*, was a national bestseller, named a *Globe and Mail* Best Book of the Year, and longlisted for the Scotiabank Giller Prize. An award-winning book designer, CS Richardson worked in publishing for forty years. He is a multiple recipient of the Alcuin Award, Canada's highest honour for excellence in book design. He lives and writes in Toronto.

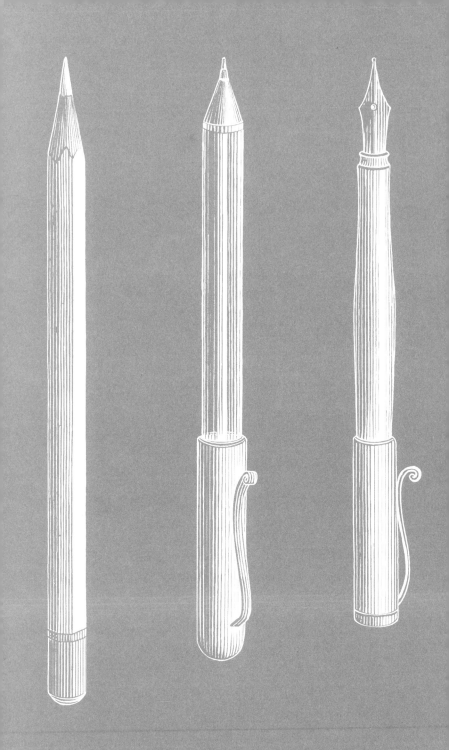